ZUKI

David Reynolds-Moreton

sci-fi-cafe.com

Zuki
David Reynolds-Moreton

sci-fi-cafe.com

Part 1
The Threat

Chapter 1
Zuki

ZUKI AWOKE FROM a dream into a living nightmare - the sounds of terrified screams, the *thunk* of metal striking something hard, and a low roaring noise. A dull, lurid red glow lit up his room as he stumbled about, trying to make sense of the cacophony of sounds which assailed his young ears.

He went to the small hole in the cottage wall which served as a window and looked out, he could see several of the little cottages with their roofs on fire, and dark shadows running about. What was happening?

The village was composed of a neat double row of well-built stone single-story dwellings, with thatched roofs, many of which were enthusiastically ablaze, while those occupants who could, ran forth, only to be mown down in a shower of arrows and the occasional spear. Those who had dodged the onslaught were then met by sword wielding creatures clad in animal skins and metal helmets – they didn't stand a chance against their attackers.

Although built of stone, the roof timbers and thatch, plus the contents, were bone dry due to the unusually hot weather, and it only needed a few sparks for the fire to spread from cottage to cottage.

Zuki ran out into what passed for a stone road between the dwellings, trying to make sense of the terrible carnage. At that moment, a blazing roof timber freed from its neighbours holding peg, swung down across the road, striking Zuki on the back of the head, and his world slipped into intense blackness as he crumpled to the ground.

One of the passing attacking creatures gave his limp body a hefty kick, but as it didn't respond, he considered it already dead, grunted, and passed on down the road, looking for anyone else still left alive.

As the grey light of dawn broke, Zuki's eyes slowly opened to be greeted by a scene he could not have imagined. Little wisps of smoke drifted up from the still smouldering timbers of what had once been a neat peaceful little row of dwellings – the occupants lay all around, some adorned with arrows, some with their heads missing, while others were so burnt as to be unrecognisable.

He slowly raised his head so as to not draw attention to himself if any of the attackers should still be around, but they were long gone – their gruesome task completed – the village had been wiped out.

Zuki rose to his feet, and swaying slightly, made his way back to the remains of his home. The stone walls still stood, but the roof and contents had all been consumed. All he could find which made any sense were the two charred bodies of his parents – he was the sole survivor.

He knew there had been bad feeling between his village and the next one, but they were only words, as far as he knew. Why kill everyone just because of a few hot words? It didn't make any sense to him. There were several disparate tribes dotted about along the foot of the great mountain, but there had never been all out war, that he knew of.

Zuki decided he should leave the village quickly, just in case the attackers returned to loot what little was left; even if they didn't return, there was little purpose in him staying here – everything was wrecked or burnt – even what little food they had.

Carefully treading between the smouldering timbers, he looked for his father's hunting knife with its sheath and belt. Fortunately for him, it had dropped down between the stone wall and the wooden water trough which had been recently filled, and so had been spared the conflagration, and there beside it was his metal drinking mug – there was precious little else worth salvaging.

Strapping on the knife belt, he looked around for the last time, gave a shuddering sigh, and strode out into road. Which way to go? To the right would lead him in the direction of the attacker's village, if it were they who had wrecked his life and that of all he had known. To the left were the orchards and animal pens – he could get some food there – if the raiders hadn't taken it all.

For a brief moment he wondered if it was worth while trying to contact the Masters, as they were referred to in the old legends, maybe they could help? – but then he thought better of it, as the Masters had tried many times to get the tribes to join them and 'become more civilised' as they put it – but everyone had refused, and so they were left to their own devices – which didn't amount to very much, according to Zuki's way of thinking.

The Masters had strange vehicles they could ride around in, which were rarely seen, and even stranger, big machines which flew around in the sky. Why his people hadn't grabbed the offer with both hands he could not fathom, although he had asked many times to be told 'their way of living was unnatural', and one day they would be punished for 'bending nature to their ways' – whatever that meant.

The animal pens had been emptied, but the fruit trees still had a good crop on them. He filled his carry bag to the brim with an assortment of fruits, but wondered what he would do for bread and meat – he knew a diet solely of fruit could have a disastrous effect on his inner working, and he didn't want that.

The stone laid road ran out just past the last orchard, to be replaced with a very faint trodden path – not many left the confines of their village as there were too many hidden dangers out there – and the stories which circulated about them didn't help much, just adding an unnecessary fear to a possible threat – which may not even exist.

Zuki looked up at the huge mountain which reached up high into the cloud base. No one had been very far up its steep slopes, as plants struggled to grow about a quarter way up, and above that was just rock. Around the base of the mountain there was a wide tract of land which supported a huge collection of plants, most of which they could use in one form or another, but after that it was just desert for as far as the eye could see. It was said that after the desert, was the land of the Masters – but no one knew for sure, as no one had been there.

Zuki had once asked why they were referred to as the Masters, as they had no impact on the tribes, and were very rarely seen. No one knew for sure, but it was suggested that a very long time ago they had been the Master race and the tribes were made to work the mines for them, but as the mines had been closed for as long as anyone could remember, it was only conjecture.

He sat down at the end of the road, not daring to try the path as he didn't know where it led. Considering his options, he began to worry; if he stayed in the village, the attackers could return; if he went up the mountain it could be only for a short way as there would be no food available up there; if he took the path at the end of the road, it might lead to another village, and they might be hostile; if he went out into the desert he would surely starve, as nothing grew there.

The only thing he could do was to go a little way along the path, and try to make some sort of shelter to protect himself from the rains which came every few days – and keep any of the many animals he had heard about from considering him to be edible. He had only seen some twelve summers, but knew he would have to grow up in a hurry if he was to survive. If only he knew how bread was made. He knew it came from the big grass seeds they all collected in the late summer, but how this was turned into bread was unknown to him. Meat he knew came from the animals they farmed, but when to kill them? And how? Anyway, he didn't like the idea of killing animals, although he had partaken of their flesh many a time.

Zuki heaved himself to his feet, looked back longingly at the orchards, turned and strode out along the faint path into the unknown.

It wasn't long before the path, such as it was, turned into a few bent blades of grass, and was then no more. Trees, and clumps of bushes were dotted about on the green sward of grass, and off to one side he could see a massive cluster of large rocks, jutting out from the landscape. Approaching the huge blocks of stone quietly in case some dangerous animal had made its home there, he peered into what looked like a black hole in one of them. If nothing else had taken advantage of this possible shelter, he would – until he could find something better.

An old, gnarled tree stood a short distance from the rocks, and it looked easy enough to climb. Zuki reasoned that if he could find some stones, climbed the tree, and then bombarded the hole in the rocks, anything therein should come out – and he would be safe up his tree – unless it could climb like him. But he had his father's hunting knife with him…a bit chancy, but what else could he do?

Finding enough large stones took a lot longer than he had expected, but he found enough in the end, and making a bag-like structure with the front of his jacket to hold them, he climbed one handed up the tree, the other hand clutching his precious stones.

The first couple of stones rattled noisily at the entrance, but the next one was on target, and went straight into the hole with a satisfying thud. A small furry animal came scurrying out, looked around, and went back into the darkness – it looked harmless enough. He had found his shelter for the night – if it was big enough for him to crawl into – and it was.

Part way in he stood up, as a bundle of fur hurried past his feet, turned to glare back at him, and then disappeared into the bushes. The nearby trees supplied him with a good supply of staves, two of which he sharpened to a fine point – if anything tried to enter his cave…The others he cut to length so that he could make a barricade at the entrance, once he was safely inside.

Zuki had seen his elders make fire by rubbing sticks together, and after a long time and very sore hands, he managed to get a little wisp of smoke from the wood dust which had collected in the grove in the main block of wood. A few dry grass blades burst into flame as he gently blew on the glowing mass, and he had his fire. A ring of stones just outside the entrance would contain his fire, and a few small dead tree stumps should last the night, with a bit of luck.

It was just turning dusk by the time he had his fire made and the staves cut to length for the barricade – and he was hungry – very hungry. He took one each of the different fruits, and ate them as slowly as he could – too many, and he would have another problem to add to the uncertainties he already had.

Sleep was long in coming that night, and when he did sleep, it was punctuated with horrific dreams of the massacre of his village. Next morning he was tired, had a raging thirst, and was sorely tempted to seek help from the Masters – if he could find them.

Zuki carefully pushed the embers of the fire together, blew on them, and added a few small twigs. He soon had a welcoming fire going which took the chill off the early morning air, and gave a little comfort to the predicament he was in – but he must find water. The village had a well, but there was no well here – maybe the animal pens had water?

Placing some sticks across the entrance to the cave so that he would know if anything had tried to get in, he set off towards the animal pens. Passing through the orchards he restocked his carry bag with fruit, ate three of the round apple-like fruits, and as the pens came into sight, and saw a small stream he hadn't noticed before.

It ran, chuckling among the stones, to a deep hole in the ground, filling it to the brim. Taking his mug from his belt, Zuki dipped it into the crystal-clear water, and drank his fill. It tasted a bit earthy, but it was wet, and slaked his not inconsiderable thirst. If only he had something to carry the water in, it would save him a long walk every time he wanted a drink, but the raiders had taken everything, except the pens themselves. Perhaps he should set up a home here? But if the raiders returned...

Zuki wearily trudged back to his cave, and then his stomach began complaining about the fruit-only diet he had subjected it to. The sticks were still in place when he checked the cave entrance, and he wondered if it was worth exploring the cave a bit more – he had only gone in a few metres last night. A bundle of thin dry sticks bound to a stake made a rudimentary torch, and lighting it, he removed the barricade of sticks and entered the dark hole.

Apart from the roundish section he had slept in, the cave continued back into a narrow tunnel, and he had to bend down to walk along it some way, when it opened out again into a round open space. The torch had burnt down almost to the carrying stick when he noticed a glimmer of light set in the cave wall ahead.

It seemed to glow with a light of its own, somehow sucking the light from the dying torch. With a final splutter, the torch went out, but the glow in the wall got brighter. What could that be? He knew some beetles glowed in the dark during the summer evenings, but this was deep in a cave – surely beetles wouldn't go deep into a cave like this?

The glow got brighter as he watched, fascinated, it seemed to light up the whole cave – and then the singing began. It wasn't singing like they did during the summer festival, it was a faint single note, clear and pure – and then it was joined by another note, and another, in perfect harmony. It was no longer a glow – it was a blaze of intense light, and it almost hurt his eyes to look at it.

Zuki felt drawn towards it, his body moving of its own accord, and his hand reached out to touch it. As his fingers made contact, a surge of energy raced up his arm, his head swam, and he slumped to the floor of the cave – unconscious.

Slowly he became aware of the cold hard floor of the cave, and then the intense blackness which surrounded him. Of the magical glow there was no sign, and the torch had gone out long ago.

Bit by bit his memory returned. He recalled entering the cave, the glow in the wall, and then the intense brightness, the singing tone, and then nothing – but there was something – he felt different somehow. The hopelessness he had felt was gone; he now knew he could survive.

Turning his head, Zuki could see the faintest glimmer of light in the distance, and crawling on hands and knees, he headed for it, but it seemed to move away from him as he scraped his knees along on the rough floor of the passage. Panic set in, he seemed to have been crawling for hours when he entered the sleeping cave of the previous night, and with a sigh of relief, he stood upright. He turned around, and in the dim light he could see the tunnel, but it seemed much smaller than before – much too small for him to have entered it – but this was impossible. He shook his head, hoping this would restore things to near normal.

Once out in the sunlight, the incident seemed like a strange dream, but somehow he knew it had been real – but what did it mean? Such things only happened in the depths of night, when he was asleep, and faded from memory in the bright light of day – but this didn't – he could remember it in all its detail.

His stomach gave a rumble, followed by a loud fart. If only he knew how to make the flat cakes he was used to, he could almost feel his teeth sinking into the crispy outer layer, and the soft gooey interior. Maybe somewhere in the ruins of the village there was just a bit of the ground up grass seeds. Ground up grass seeds? How did he know they were ground up...

It didn't take long to reach the remains of what had once been a cosy little village, but now only the stone walls were left, and a dreadful stench filled the air as the dead bodies began to decompose in the heat of the sun. Zuki hurried from ruin to ruin, searching for the big clay pots the flour was usually kept in, but they had either been taken by the raiders, or destroyed in the dreadful blaze which had wreaked his world.

And then he remembered, his mother kept the flour in a small lean-to at the back of the cottage as it was cooler there, and the flour didn't go sour – could it have escaped the fire?

The lean-to being built of stone had escaped the worst of the blaze, as the roof was made of thin planks of wood and not thatch, and had quickly burnt up. Sure enough, the big pot was there, a heap of ash covering the lid. Some of the flour had turned brown where it was next to the surface of the pot, but the rest looked a pale honey colour as it should be.

With the big pot under his arm, he returned to his cave in the wooded area past the orchards, adding some water to his mug as he passed the pool by the pens. Now he could make bread, but what about meat? He knew he should eat it, but still didn't like the idea of killing an animal to do so. But there were no animals left in the pens, so that only left the wild ones – so which were edible? And how could he catch and kill them? Somehow, he knew he would find the answer when the time came to do so.

But how did he know that? Each question rarely had an answer, and seemed to spawn more questions…

Zuki tasted some of the dark brown flour at the edge of the pot – it had a pleasant nutty flavour, so he mixed it with the normal flour – he wasn't going to waste anything. He drank some of the water, leaving what he thought was the right amount to mix with the flour to make a dough, as he had seen his mother do so many times.

With the fire stoked up, he let it burn down to hot embers, found a large flat stone, and placed it on the glowing embers, arranging the flattened little disks of dough on its surface.

When one side was browned, he flipped them over, eagerly waiting for the other side to do likewise – and then he had his bread. But it didn't taste like the flat cakes his mother made. She must have added something else to the mixture, but what? At least it would augment his fruit diet, and perhaps settle his grumbling stomach and frequent visits to the bushes.

As the evening drew in, he stoked up his fire, and began to think of the meat and vegetable stews his mother used to make; sometimes she would drop in some of the flat cake dough mixture, and this produced fluffy soft balls with a delicious taste, and his mouth began to salivate. He didn't know where the vegetables came from – except for a few which he had seen growing in one of the fields, but meat was going to be the main problem.

As the evening deepened into night the stars came out, along with the rustles and squeaks of the night creatures. Drowsiness eventually overcame Zuki, and he decided to retire to his cave, but first he put a large dead tree stump on the fire with a few twigs in front to light up the entrance of the cave and his bundle of blocking staves.

Once inside, he could see in the flickering firelight, the tiny entrance to the tunnel he had crawled out of earlier. No way could he get into it now, so how come it had shrunk? There was something magical about the whole affair – but he didn't believe in magic, so what was going on?

Finally his eyes closed, and he slept deeply – no nasty nightmares, just a deep sleep from which he awoke feeling fully refreshed. It was early morning, the stars winking out one by one, and a rosy glow on the horizon. Somehow, he felt today was going to be different.

A couple of flat cakes left over from last night and some fruit satiated the grumblings of an empty stomach, but did little to prevent the copious amounts of wind he was producing. If he was going to go hunting for meat, this could be a hindrance as the silence could be inadvertently broken at any moment, so giving him away.

Zuki got to thinking about the desert – was it so very bad that it couldn't be crossed? And did the Masters really live on the other side of it? Also, would they help him if he found them? He only had the stories he had heard to go by, and some of those stories were just too silly to be true – so were they all based on old superstitions? He decided to have a look at the desert for himself, and base his actions on facts.

To this end, he baked all the flour into flat cakes, placing them at the bottom of his carry bag, with the fruit on top. He thought if he was careful with his rations, they should last several days, and when he had consumed half of them, he would turn back and return to his cave. Water was going to be his main problem, as he only had the empty flour container to carry it in, and that didn't amount to a great volume. A thin vine provided a sling to hold his water supply pot, and after filling it, he was almost ready to go.

With the fire raked out, the staves blocking off the cave entrance and a few leafy branches draped over them as a camouflage, Zuki left his camp and headed south towards where he thought the desert lay.

At first the going was easy, but then the trees began to thicken in numbers, and he had to forget about going in a straight path, snaking between the forest giants as best he could. Huge vines hung down from the massive branches high above him, some adorned with the most beautiful flowers he had ever seen, and a heavy scent hung in the air making him feel sleepy. Several of the giant trees had a little pile of white sticks around their bases, and he wondered how they got there.

Zuki's inquisitive nature had often got him into trouble, and he couldn't resist a challenge. He went over to one pile of sticks, and realised that some had broken down to a crumbly mess, while others seemed to be new and in good condition – and then it dawned on him, they were bones – he recognised them from the leftovers of many a meal, but these were only small bones.

It looked as if small creatures, when they felt near to their end, lay down around the tree's base to die – but why would they do that? He realised something else was going on, but couldn't fathom just what it was. And then the token dropped, as they say. He had felt sleepy, and could quite happily lay down for a sleep – it must be the scent from the flowers. Perhaps the trees needed something from the animal's dead bodies which they couldn't get any other way, and let the creepers grow on them in exchange for their sleepy scent – yes, that made sense, so he hurried away from the flower draped vines as fast as he could.

As Zuki moved through the forest, he carefully avoided any flowers or anything else which smelled nice, just in case it was a trap. He had been going for some time when he noticed the huge trees were not quite so huge, and they were a little more spaced apart. Bushes were now interspersed with the trees, and then the trees were no more – just clumps of bushes of different sorts, but the grass was still present - then that got sparser – just little patches, and then the desert came into view.

Like huge rolling waves of sand and small stones, the desert stretched off into the distance for as far as he could see, blending in with the far horizon in a hazy blur. The odd bush broke up the monotony of the barren land for a while, and then they too were gone – just sand, and more sand.

He had been very careful with his water supply, topping it up from a pool just before he had left the trees, but now he felt thirsty as the sun beat down relentlessly. A small sip, just to keep his mouth wet was all he allowed himself, until he stopped for a meal. He trudged on, but it was hard work walking over the sand as his feet sank in with each step, and now his legs began to ache – time for a break, and a little sustenance.

Zuki turned around to see how far he had travelled, but there was no sign of the forest – just a blur on the horizon – he felt a flash of fear – suppose he couldn't find his way back? But of course he could, just keep the sun at his back – the fear faded away as he sat down to enjoy some fruit and one of his precious flat cakes, and then a good mouthful of water – although it was warm, it was very soothing, and he was tempted to take another swig – no, he must make it last.

He had only been walking for a short while, when he noticed a movement of something up ahead. Surely nothing lived out here? But something did, and it was moving. Zuki climbed the next ridge and looked down on a nightmare. The creature was twice his height in length, with a fat scaly body and a long whip-like tail, on the end of which was a barbed point. He froze – had it seen him? He wanted to race back down the slope behind him, but knew any movement would attract its attention.

He could feel his legs beginning to shake, and tried to relax them. Could he outrun the creature if it decided he looked like a meal? He doubted it, four sturdy legs held it off the scorching sand, and they were well muscled. The head slowly swung around in his direction, two jet black eyes surveying the area for something to eat.

Out of the corner of his eye, he saw another movement; a beetle shaped thing about the size of his head had just emerged from the sand, and as its twin antenna swung around to orientate itself, the whip-like tail of the lizard creature flicked out in one clean and precise movement to impale the beetle on the barbed end. The tail then swung around to deposit the beetle in its slit-like mouth, and Zuki could clearly hear the crunch as the powerful jaws crushed the beetle's carapace into fragments. One gulp, and the beetle was gone.

He was tempted to empty his stock of fruit and cakes out onto the sand, and then run for it, but then realised the creature probably only recognised live food, and would go after him instead. While still desperately thinking of what to do, the creature tucked its head into the sand and wriggled its way beneath the surface, to find a cooler layer in which to digest its meal.

Zuki slowly backed down the sandy ridge, and went along its bottom for some distance before venturing up again to see if anything else was on the move. All was still, except for a small stone which rolled down the slope before settling in its new position on the barren landscape.

The lizard thing was totally unexpected, and he wondered how many of them might exist out here in the wilderness. There was nothing for it, he must plod on to find the Masters.

The sun dipped down below the horizon, and the temperature dropped. Zuki chose a deep hollow in the sand for the night, just in case a wind got up due to the temperature change, and he was proved right. The meal, as frugal as it was, calmed him down a little, and he was just about to curl up and rest his aching body when something shiny, high up in the sky caught his eye. It couldn't be a star as it was moving, and at quite a speed – was this one of the flying things he had heard about? Perhaps the Masters were real after all.

Strangely, he didn't dream that night, but dawn came all too soon. A quick meal, a drink from his dwindling water supply, and he was off again. Two more cycles of the sun, and his water was half gone. He knew he should turn back to ensure his survival, but then it would have all been in vain, and he had no idea of how much further he would have to travel to find the Masters.

***

The patrol vessel skimmed across the barren wastes, a mere two metres above its scorching surface, the pilot steering a predetermined course set by the Bureau for Outland Control. The system had been set up many years ago to prevent citizens from roaming the barren wastes looking for precious gems – none were found, but rumours persisted despite this, and people went missing. It had been a long time since the patrol had actually been needed – no one with any sense would venture out there now, but no one had cancelled the patrols – if nothing else, it gave some people a not too arduous job to do – but its days were numbered.

'Hey, look down there,' the navigator said, 'looks like someone has wandered out into the desert.'

The pilot swung the craft off course and gained a little more height so that they could see what was down on the rolling dunes.

'Looks like a small boy, I would think,' said the navigator, 'what the hell's he doing out here?'

'More to the point, how did he get here?' the pilot replied, 'there's no sign of a vehicle, and he couldn't have done it on foot. Do you want to go down and see what he's up to?'

'Better had – this is the first time we've seen anyone out here in years.'

The craft swung around and dropped height to land a few metres from the lone figure on the sands.

'Hey boy, what are you doing, and how did you get here?' the navigator asked.

'I am looking for the Masters,' Zuki replied, when the shock of seeing the flying machine had passed. 'My village has been destroyed by another tribe, and I'm all that's left – they killed everyone and burnt the village down.'

'Who are these Masters you refer to?' asked the pilot, 'I've never heard of them – where do they live?'

'On the other side of the desert, so I've been told,' Zuki replied, 'they are the clever people who wanted us to join them, but our elders refused. They have all sorts of wonderful things, but our elders said they were not living naturally, and didn't want to join them. Now I'm the only one left, and I have no where to live.'

'We can't leave the poor little sod out here, he'll die of heat exhaustion, that's if the sand lizards don't get him first,' the navigator quietly said to the pilot, 'we could take him back with us, and let the authorities sort it out.'

The navigator nodded his assent.

'Exactly where have you come from?' asked the pilot, still not believing anyone could have walked out this far into the desert.

'I lived in a village by the foot of the great mountain – there are lots of tribes like ours, but some are very cruel, and one attacked us a few nights ago.' Zuki said, wondering just who these men were.

'Why don't you join one of the other tribes?' asked the navigator, 'you would be more at home with your own kind of people.'

'I don't know which one would have me, I might be killed if they don't like me, that's why I'm looking for the Masters – they are supposed to be kind people.' Zuki said firmly.

'OK son, we could take you back with us, and try to find you a home with some nice people, if that's what you want,' the navigator said, 'I don't know who these Masters are, but it might be us you refer to – we don't know of any other people, except the tribes who live around the mountain you mentioned.'

'You mean you are the Masters?' Zuki said in a voice filled with awe, 'and you could give me a home?'

'That's about the size of it, son,' the pilot replied, 'you'll die if we leave you out here, anyway, what's your name?'

'Zuki' he replied with a sigh of relief, 'and thank you very much.' The pilot just nodded, with a smile.

'It'll be a bit of a squeeze,' he said, 'these craft are only meant for two, and that's a bit tight if one of us is a little overweight,' indicating the navigator with a grin.

They managed to squeeze Zuki in behind the pair of them, as there were only two seats, and the craft rose silently up into the air, turned, and headed out over the desert towards the land of the 'Masters'.

The desert land rolled past under them, wave after wave of boiling hot sand and gravel until they came to the first sign of greenery. It began with a few dried-up looking bushes, then patches of grass followed by trees, but not like the ones Zuki was used to.

'What are those?' asked Zuki, pointing at the neat rows of trees which seemed to go on right out to the horizon.

'That's where we grow our fruit,' said the pilot.

'That's an awful lot of trees.' Zuki responded.

'There are an awful lot of people eating it,' he replied with a grin, 'just you wait 'till you see the size of our villages.'

At long last the trees gave way to huge open fields, some were just grass, but others where growing multi-coloured crops, the like of which Zuki had never seen before.

And then the town came into view. Some of the buildings were made of a glistening white stone, while others clad in a glassy material reached up to the clouds themselves. Zuki craned forward and thrust his head between that of the other two, just to get a better view.

'You think this is big, just you wait 'till you see our capital city,' said the pilot grinning, 'that will make your eyes pop out.'

The craft lost height, and came to a gentle rest beside one of the huge white buildings.

'This is where we get out,' said the pilot, 'and try and find you a home.'

The three of them entered the building, the navigator leading the way to a lift, which left Zuki gasping for breath as it sped up-shaft in as many seconds as there were floors, and there were eighteen of them.

While the pilot stayed with Zuki, the navigator went from office to office, trying to sort out just who would be responsible for their new charge. After many video calls to those in high office, it was decided that if the navigator wished, Zuki could be bonded to him, and a small grant of credits would be given to him to cover his extra expenses.

A long explanation to his life partner over a video link, and it was agreed that Zuki could join the family unit. When this was explained to Zuki, his first comment was,

'Does this mean you will be my father?'

'Well, not exactly, but to all intents and purposes, I will be. You can call me Dunn.'

The pilot bid the pair goodbye and left. Zuki and Dunn returned to the lift, while Zuki held his breath as it plummeted down to ground level, and then let it out with a great whoosh, much to the amusement of Dunn.

The journey to Dunn's apartment was in a similar version of the craft which had rescued Zuki from the desert, except it was a little roomier and with comfortable seats. When they met Dunn's partner, she inquired what he had in his carry bag. Zuki proudly put the contents on a table, explaining he had made the flat cakes himself, and offered one to her. She took a small bite, and her face could not hide the fact that the cake lacked salt and sugar, which she explained to him in a gentle manner; Zuki said that he knew they were not quite a good as those made by his mother, but he didn't know what else to put in them.

He was shown to his room, and marvelled at the comfort of his bed, explaining that he had slept on a straw mattress, and thought that was a good as a bed could be.

Over the next few days, Zuki was taken around the city, fitted out with new clothes, and introduced to a school, but he had to begin at a very low level as he had no knowledge of writing or mathematics. What surprised his teacher was the speed with which he absorbed data, and seemed to understand it.

Twenty days into his intensive learning, and he was up to his age group, and joined a regular class.

Chee (Dunn's partner) grew fond of the young boy, and spent many an hour helping him with his learning, but was soon left behind as science was added to the curriculum. It wasn't long before Zuki realised that he was different to the other pupils, especially in his learning ability, and decided to try and hide it, as he didn't want to appear different.

Academy followed school, and the degrees came thick and fast.

'What sort of child did you bring back from the desert?' Chee asked her partner, one day, 'I'm sure the others of his tribe were not like him, or they would have advanced well beyond the simple life they seem to have.'

'I was wondering that,' Dunn replied, 'he's a very likable lad, but as you say, there is something strange about him; he often asks me questions I can't answer, and that is embarrassing.' She chuckled; she had felt the same.

One day Zuki asked about the old stories of the Masters using the tribes to work in the mines. At first, his new parents were unable to answer his queries, as they knew little about them – so Dunn went to the Archives to find out. After much searching, and some funny looks from those in charge, he was called to the main office of the Archivist.

An elderly, stern-looking man enquired why Dunn was so interested in such things which had happened so long ago.

'I have a son who is interested in our past, and I am unable to answer his questions. The archives don't reveal very much, it would seem such data is restricted.'

'Hmm,' came the reply, 'some data is restricted as it is thought unnecessary for general use. We only have written data going back four hundred years or so, all our old records were destroyed when a large meteorite struck part of the city. Bring the boy in tomorrow, and I'll see what I can do.'

When Zuki was told of the coming visit to the Archives, he felt a surge of excitement, but didn't know why.

'I've often wondered about the Masters and our tribes,' he said, 'I know it's only based on the old tales the elders sometimes talk about, but there must be something in it for it to persist for so long. Why didn't our tribes accept the Master's offer of help? It seems silly not to, when you look at all the wonderful things you have. And how come there are two lots of people on our world – they must have been one race at some time in the past surely.'

'I don't know, son, we'll find out tomorrow, with a bit of luck – I must say, I am getting interested in it now.' Dunn replied, with an eagerness which surprised him.

The following day the pair went to the Archive building and were ushered into the main archive office, and greeted by the same man as the day before.

'I have been digging up some of the old records which go way back, and although not for public usage, I have extracted quite a lot of information from them,' said the man behind the big desk, 'but there is one more piece of data I have one of my researchers still looking for, and he will bring it in, if he can find it. So, what exactly do you two want to know?'

Dunn didn't know quite what to ask, but Zuki was ready with a stream of questions,

'Were we all one race at one time?' he asked eagerly.

'Yes,' replied the chief archivist, 'it would seem so, but for some reason a group of religious fanatics broke away from the main population, and sought peace and quiet out in the barren lands. Over time, due to the conditions and different food stuffs, they changed in stature and appearance, and in time looked like a different race to us, but were genetically the same.'

'Is it true that you people, the Masters, used them to do mining work for you, and what was it they mined?' asked Zuki, eagerly leaning forward.

'Yes, it would appear so, they were better accustomed to the conditions prevailing in the barren lands than we were,' the man replied, 'but what they were mining is the bit of information I am trying to get – for some reason, it has been made very difficult to obtain.'

'Why do you think my people didn't join you when asked to do so?'

'That is something we don't know – there were, according to the records, many attempts to amalgamate the two groups, but they refused for some obscure reason, so we gave up in the end and let them get on with it. We considered it would be unethical to use force.'

'The people of the barren lands refer to you as the 'Masters' in their legends, is that because you made them work in the mines?' asked Zuki.

'I would think so, but we don't refer to ourselves as the Masters.' The man at the desk said, looking a bit uncomfortable.

At that moment there was knock at the door, and a young man entered.

'I think this is what you are looking for, sir,' he said, handing over a very old piece of age browned paper, 'I had one hell of a job to get it, and had to lie in order to do so.'

'Don't worry, I'll find some sort of excuse to cover you, if the need arises,' the archivist said, 'and thanks for your work.'

Slowly and carefully, the old piece of paper was laid flat. It looked more like a piece of well-worn parchment than paper, and the archivist was having trouble reading it.

'From what I can make out,' he began, hesitatingly, 'the miners were instructed to dig a tunnel into the mountain, and if they came across a glittering crystal, they had to call one of us. The miners were then moved back some way, and our man put a box-like thing over the crystal, and somehow it was manoeuvred into the box, and taken away.' He moved closer, and screwed his eyes up as if trying to get them into focus on the faded writing.

'It would seem that the crystals were very highly prized, but no one was allowed to look at them – they had to be kept in their box, and no light was allowed to fall on them – somehow, that was very important.'

'What do you think the crystals were used for?' asked Zuki, an idea already forming in his mind, as he recalled what happened to him at the back of the cave he had slept in.

'Don't know,' the man replied, 'it doesn't say what they were used for here, but they were only moved about the place with an armed guard, they must have been considered very valuable to someone.'

'What would happen if you looked at one of them?' asked Zuki, half knowing the answer, but not saying anything about the experience he had had.

'I don't know, it doesn't say anything about looking at the crystals here, except they must only be exposed to light when they are used – but it doesn't say for what.'

The archivist squinted his eyes yet again, trying to decipher the faint writing, but apart from a few grunts, nothing else was forthcoming.

'You seem very interested in these crystals,' the archivist said at last, his voice indicating that Zuki knew a little more that he was saying.

'The old legends tell of something magical in the mines,' Zuki replied, 'I just wondered what it was, and if it was worth looking for.'

'Have any of your people been in the mines of late?' the archivist asked, his interest picking up.

'No, I've never heard of anyone doing that,' Zuki answered, 'I don't think anyone has been there for several generations – it's only mentioned when someone is telling one of the old tales.'

The archivist gave him a long hard cold stare, before asking the next question:

'I think you know something about these crystals which you aren't telling us – so what is it?'

'I just wondered what they were used for, and why the mining stopped when they were so valuable.' Zuki replied, realising he had already said too much.

'But you didn't know a lot of this until I told you,' The archivist said knowingly, 'so what do you know that we don't? Are you sure they aren't looking for crystals again?'

'Yes, absolutely sure, they won't go near the mines – they think they're cursed.' Zuki said, hoping the subject would be dropped.

'And did you hear that in one of the tales?'

'Yes,' Zuki said, lamely.

'Hmm,' said the archivist, after a long pause, 'there is nothing else I can tell you from this old document that makes any sense, so we'll leave it at that for now, but I expect someone will contact you in the future, just in case your memory improves a little.' He added.

As the meeting had drawn to a somewhat strained close, Dunn and Zuki left and headed home, Dunn saying very little until they were indoors.

'OK, so what do you know that you didn't tell the archivist? Asked Dunn, 'things don't add up. You are from a rather simple people, and yet you learn at a prodigious rate, far outstripping your classmates. You are very curious about something that has been long forgotten. Why?'

'If I tell you, will you promise not to tell anyone else?' asked Zuki, hoping he could trust his adoptive father.

'Alright, I promise, as long as it will not harm any of us.' Dunn replied, sinking backing his chair.

Zuki told him about the cave, the strange crystal glow, and what happened to him when he exposed it to the light of the torch.

'It would seem it has changed you, somehow, although I don't understand how,' Dunn said after a moments silence, as he absorbed the enormity of what had happened, 'I agree, you shouldn't tell anyone about this until you feel it is safe to do so. I think the old archivist knows something is going on, but I don't think he has figured out just what it is.'

'Do you think he will tell others?' asked Zuki, anxiously, 'And will they question me?'

'No, I don't think so, at least not at the moment. You will have to hide your new skills if possible. Learn all you can, and when it comes to exams, do moderately well so you don't stand out too much. I think I can see what these crystals do, but I don't know how they do it.' Dunn sighed. He was now getting involved in something he felt was very powerful, and possibly dangerous.

Time went by. Zuki finished his schooling, the advanced academy, and much to Dunn and Chee's disappointment, signed up for flight school – he wanted to fly the big machines he had seen cruising about the sky - nearly every boy's dream.

His skill as a pilot soon became apparent, and he was singled out for the more difficult jobs after graduating flight school, and joined one of the big freighting companies. But this wasn't going to last very long.

Chapter 2
The Proposition

He was on home leave, when Dunn answered the musical tone of the door annunciator. A tall thin man in what amounted to a discrete uniform stood there, smiled, and asked if he could come in.

They joined Zuki and Chee in the main living room, and after introductions, sat down.

'What I am about to say must remain within these four walls. It is most definitely not for public consumption. Do you all agree to this?' The tall, thin man sat back in his chair, to judge how the others reacted.

Dun and Chee looked at each other, and then at Zuki, who nodded his head.

'I suppose this is about our son.' said Dunn.

'Yes, it is,' replied the man, 'but it also involves you two as well, to some extent – let me explain. You obviously know we have a space programme, and visit other worlds in our solar system. We think your son would be ideal as a ship's pilot. It would mean you all signing a security clause with extreme penalties if it were broken – you need to really think about this. Once signed, there is no going back.'

'This seems very dramatic,' said Dunn, wondering what it was all about, 'we know our lad is very bright, and we know about space flight, so why the security? Such things are common knowledge.'

'There is a little more than normal space flight involved here. We have detected a possible threat to our system, and we want the very best people in our team. You must have realised that your son has certain talents most people don't have, and we think we can use these talents, if he would be willing to join us. It is not without danger, but we will take very good care of him – it is in our interests to do so.'

The silence which followed was almost palpable, except for the artificial ticking sound of the electronic clock on the wall.

'What do you think, Zuki?' asked Dunn.

Chee started to rise from her chair. Her son seemed paralysed, even his chest wasn't moving, and she began to panic. A restraining hand from Dunn held her back.

'It's OK Chee, he's got to work this out on his own, he's alright. I've seen this before.'

The moments dragged by, and then with a deep sigh, Zuki began to breathe again.

'I would like to join your team,' Zuki said firmly, turning to look directly at the man, 'You know I can't refuse.'

'Thank you,' the man responded, with a smile. Turning to Dunn and Chee, he added 'are you two both in agreement with Zuki? Do you have anything else you would like to ask?'

'No, not really. We both know he is something special,' Dunn replied, 'just flying freight around couldn't last for long, we knew that, but what you have said is a bit of a surprise. Anyway, how long have you been watching Zuki?'

'For quite some time, in fact ever since he was at junior school,' the man replied, 'he stood out as someone exceptional.'

'Are there others like Zuki?' asked Chee, hoping he would be with others of like kind.

'No, not really. He has, we think, some exceptional talents. We will have to see just what he is capable of,' the man said, 'but I don't think we will be disappointed.'

'When will this take place?' asked Dunn, fearing they would lose their adopted son.

'In a couple of days,' he replied, 'we will have to square things up with the freight company, I don't expect they will want to lose him, and then he will join our unit. He will of course get leave to visit you, but not for a while. We will, however, keep you informed of his progress – well, as much as we are able to under the circumstances. By the way, my name is Brond, you can contact me using this,' handing Dunn a small plastic card.

'I will leave you now,' Brond said, 'think over carefully that which I have told you, and if you are in full agreement, sign the papers which will be delivered to you in a day or so. You can back out of this, but I sincerely hope you won't.'

With that, Brond arose from his seat, shook hands with all present, and left.

'Are you sure you want to do this, Zuki?' asked Chee, a look of apprehension on her face.

'Yes mother, somehow I know I must – I can't explain it, but it feels right.' And then he told her what he had told his father about the strange crystal in the cave.

'What worries me,' said Dunn, 'is if we refuse to let Zuki go, knowing what the man told us, how can they be sure we won't talk?'

The following day two men arrived, introduced themselves, and asked Dunn and Chee to sign the papers which committed them to total silence about Zuki, took DNA swabs, and left.

'Things are moving just a little bit too fast for comfort,' said Dunn, 'can't say I like it very much.' Chee just nodded.

Two days later, and they had another visit from Brond.

'Are you ready, young man?' he asked, 'It is time to go. Say your goodbyes to your parents please, we have much to do.'

Zuki hugged his father, and then his mother, noticing her eyes were wet.

'I'll be in touch as much as I can, and I'll get leave when the time is right.'

One part of his life was ending, and another about to begin.

Outside the house was a land cruiser, its door opening as the pair approached. A soft whine, and they were heading off down the street which had become Zuki's home for so many years, and he wondered what the future held for him.

'Things may not be quite what you may have been expecting,' said Brond, as the cruiser lifted into the air, 'we must first determine just what your talents are, and how much control you have over them. This will be something new for me as well as you, as we have never had anyone quite like you to work with before.'

If this was meant to instil a feeling of calm in Zuki, it failed completely.

'Where are we going?' he asked nervously, 'I didn't even know a land cruiser could fly.'

'Normally they don't,' replied Brond, 'but this is a rather special one, as are many things you will see in the future.'

The cruiser left the city, and suddenly gained height, disappearing into the cloud base. They were surrounded by an all-enveloping thick white mist, and Zuki felt uneasy as he couldn't see where they were going.

'Don't look so worried,' said Brond, 'we are flying on a preset course through a controlled zone, not like your freighters. We'll be there soon.'

Suddenly, the craft dropped out of the cloud layer to reveal a basin shaped valley in the middle of a circular mountain range. The cruiser spiralled down to a clear space in the middle of the basin, and came to rest in a cloud of dust. There was a lurch, and the craft slowly sank down a shaft to a huge, cavernous area, and the top of the shaft closed over – the landing area in the mountain was once more sand, rock, and not a mark to show that anything had happened, apart from a very large bird with a wickedly curved beak circling high overhead.

'Well, we're here,' said Brond cheerfully, 'we'll fix you up with some quarters, and then I'll take you around the complex and explain things – tomorrow we begin the real work.'

Although Zuki felt wide awake when he retired to his quarters for the night, as soon as his head hit the pillow he fell into a deep sleep, waking next day to the sound of a distant bell. He had no sooner washed and dressed, when a knock on his door and a cheerful 'good morning' signalled the arrival of Brond.

'After a quick meal to get your energy levels up, we will begin the tests.' It sounded more like a command than a request, Zuki thought.

The food, although it didn't look very appetising, tasted good, and then they were on their way to the test facility. Down seemingly endless corridors and a couple of lifts, they reached the assessment area.

'On the screen in front of you, numbers will be flashed up randomly, in different positions, and they will only be visible for a fraction of a second. You job is to add them up, and give me the total at the end of the test,' said Brond, 'this is to test your response time and overall spatial awareness.'

A series of faint flashes of light lit up the screen for a moment, and then were gone.

'What number do you have?' asked Brond.

'57,812.' Zuki replied.

'Thank you. That is correct, and astonishing,' Brond said, dumbfounded, 'all I saw were a few faint flashes of light. There were over six thousand numbers, and you got every one of them. Before this, I would have said that was impossible – well done.'

'The next test may be a little more unpleasant,' Brond said, 'it involves a simulation of a dangerous environment. You have to work your way through to the end. No harm will come to you, but it will feel very real. It uses holograms to generate a situation which is normally life threatening. This will test your ability to react quickly and decisively, judging which threat is the greater, and avoiding it. Are you willing to do this?'

For a brief moment the terrible scene of the attack on his village flashed through his mind, restimulated by the thought of a threatening situation, and then it was gone.

'Yes,' replied Zuki, 'I think I can differentiate between that which is real and a simulation.'

'I wouldn't be too sure of that,' Brond said grimly, 'we have gone to great lengths to make it seem real.'

They left the room, and went into a long dark passageway, Zuki was told to stand perfectly still while the system located him, and then it began.

He was in a bitterly cold tunnel of ice, with a freezing wind howling at his back, almost pushing him off his feet. A series of dark holes in the floor made going forward seem like suicide, but he would have to, as huge icicles began to randomly fall from the ceiling above, any of which if they had struck him, would have impaled him to the ice floor.

He felt a searing pain in his right shoulder as one icicle just grazed him to shatter into razor sharp fragments on the floor of the tunnel. He noticed that the icicles gave a little ticking sound before they fell, so using this, he was able to jump between the holes in the floor and the potentially falling icicles to proceed down the tunnel.

And now the icy cold blast of air behind him seemed to warm, and then it was hot – so hot he could smell his jacket singeing. The ice above him was also melting, forming big puddles between the ever-enlarging holes in the floor of the tunnel. Zuki quickly threw himself down on the wet floor to put out the burning jacket, while the ice seemed to melt all at once.

The tunnel quickly flooded, and he had to swim in the ever-deepening water. Soon it was up to roof level, and he was running out of air. He noticed there were small indentations in the tunnel roof – small pockets of air – he swam forward, turning on his back as each air pocket drew level – a quick gasp of air, and he swam on to the next one.

Then he was out of the tunnel – before him was an arid landscape of rocks and gravel, but the light had dimmed, and it was difficult to make out any fine detail.

A cross between a hiss and a roar drew his attention up ahead. A huge lizard-like creature was baring his path, its tongue flicking out to scent the air for anything edible. Between him and the lizard was a bear-like animal, which emitted a loud snarl and bared twin tusks as soon as it saw him. In front of that, was a huge snake, coiled up, with its head swaying around in a hypnotizing dance. Just in front of Zuki, a small fluffy creature somewhat like a rabbit which sat up and looked at him, its big floppy ears dangling down almost to the ground, its large blue eyes locked onto his, begging him not to do what he knew he must.

Zuki quickly stooped down, grabbed the rabbit and threw it at the snake. The snake's head swung around and caught the rabbit in mid air, but Zuki waited until the snake had half swallowed the rabbit before he leaped forward, grabbed the snake and threw it at the bear thing. The coils of the snake wrapped around the bear, and began to choke it. The bear responded by reaching out with both clawed paws to grip the snakes head, and bit it off.

The coils continued to tighten on the bear and then Zuki ran forward, leaped onto the bears back, and gripping the head, wrenched it back, snapping its neck. He now retreated a few paces as the lizard came forward, tongue flickering out to pick up the bears scent – and the great jaws opened revealing a double row of sharp teeth. As the jaws clamped down on the bear, Zuki ran forward and leapt over the lizard and onto the path ahead, running as fast as he could, and then skidded to a halt.

Ahead of him five humanoid creatures dressed in animal skins and with metal helmets on their heads stood in a row, blocking his path. Each had a spear, and one raised its arm to launch it. Zuki could hear it whistle as it cleaved the air between them, and then time slowed down, or seemed to. The flight of the spear decreased to a point where he could deflect it to one side as it neared him, and then the others raised their arms, and four more spears flew towards him.

He dropped to the ground as the spears whistled over his head, and grabbed a handful of sand. Leaping to his feet, Zuki ran for the humanoid in the middle, throwing the sand in its face as he neared it. The blood curdling scream which followed almost stopped him in his tracks, but he forced his over worked muscles to drive him past the humanoids, and on down the path. Suddenly there was a blaze of light, and he was back in the passageway with Brond.

Zuki was soaked in sweat and shaking.

'I really didn't think you would get through that lot in one piece,' said Brond, giving him a pat on the back. 'That proved several points. One, you can collate data at a phenomenal rate, and make the right decision. Two, you can accurately gauge a possible dangerous action to get you out of trouble, and sequence it correctly. And three, you can override your normal emotional response if the situation calls for an apparent cruel action to aid your own survival. I wonder what other skills you have tucked away at the back of your mind. Come on young man, I think some refreshments are called for.'

'You were right,' said Zuki, as they walked down the passageway, 'that was as real as anything I have experienced in the past. How did the machine pull memories from my mind, and put them into the scene?'

'That I don't know, I'm not a technician,' Brond replied, 'but it's a clever bit of kit.'

'How many others have been through that machine, and come out OK?' asked Zuki.

'Only two others have similar talents as you do – not quite the same, but very useful in difficult situations. Only one is alive at the moment, and he is far from here.'

Zuki wanted to ask what happened to the other one, but as the data wasn't offered, he thought it probably wouldn't be given anyway.

The canteen was reached, and they helped themselves to food and drink, sitting down opposite each other.

'What is this threat to our solar system you mentioned earlier?' asked Zuki.

'Well, I can tell you quite a bit about it, but not all at the moment,' Brond said, lowering his voice a little, 'As you may know, we visit several planets in our system for rare earth metals, and on the furthest one out we found that our mining operation had been shut down, and all the workers had been killed, although there were no signs of bodily damage, like a wound, so we put it down to some kind of radiation. Much later we found they had been killed by some form of neutron bombardment. It kills all life forms, but doesn't destroy material things, like buildings and other structures.

Some raiders from outside our system had attacked our operation, and could now pose a threat to us. We had an encounter with aliens some time ago, and we won the battle, but not without heavy losses. This lot seem to be a bit different, as far as we can tell, so we don't know what we're up against. Their weapons seem similar to ours, so we could just slog it out, and I think we would win, but the cost would be very high. We need something else to force them out of our system, and discourage them from ever returning again. I think we may have that something, and that's where you come in.' Brond paused for breath.

'But I don't have any fighting skills,' said Zuki, 'so what use could I be?'

'We don't need fighters, we have plenty of them – what we need is someone who is not affected by just about anything. No, that's not quite right. We need someone with mental skills none of us have, and I think you might be that person.'

Zuki looked puzzled. He still couldn't see what use he could be.

'Let me explain a bit more,' Brond said after a moment, 'in our first encounter, we managed to capture one of the aliens alive – and in a way, wished we hadn't. One of our men interrogated the alien, but as he wasn't getting anywhere. He applied a little more pressure than we normally allow, shall we say? The upshot of that was that the alien went into some sort of mental overload, blew his mind and that of the interrogator as well. The poor man is now marooned on one of our outer planets, and no one can go near him.'

'Why not?' asked Zuki, 'is he aggressive or something?'

'No, nothing so simple,' Brond replied, 'he has a mental stink about him which we can't stand. It's hard to explain, but the slightest threat or upset, and he radiates out some sort of mental wave which makes us nauseous. And I don't mean just feeling sick – I mean vomit 'till there's nothing left, and then trying to bring that up.

Before we got things under some sort of control, several people died from shear exhaustion. In the end we had to tranquillise him, and that only reduced the mental wave to one that was just bearable. Our best medics tried everything, but nothing worked, so we had to isolate him. That stressed him out, and a few more died. In the end we had to ship the poor sod out to an uninhabited planet under heavy sedation – with plenty of supplies, and they are topped up using a remote-controlled delivery system.'

Zuki looked shocked, didn't speak for a while, and then said,

'I don't see where I come in – what can I do?'

'There's just a chance you might be able to withstand what he's radiating, and so try to get him to help us. What he does may affect the aliens also, and that could be our most potent weapon. We've tried radio communication, but he's not having anything to do with it – can't blame him, I'd feel the same.'

'But how do you know it won't affect me?' asked Zuki.

'The short answer is, we don't. We can't duplicate the mental wave he emits, so there's no way of testing you – I know it's a big ask, but would you give it a try?'

'I still don't see how that would help you.' said Zuki.

'This new bunch of aliens have wiped out a mining operation on one of the outer planets, as I said earlier. So, we sent observation probes out to see what they would do next. They sent a ship to the planet where our 'stinky man' is; it circled around for a while, and then landed near his dwelling. Next thing we knew, it took off at a high rate of knots, leaving several of its crew behind. A vision probe showed their remains – it looked as if they had tried to turn themselves inside out. It was a disgusting mess. Obviously, they must have frightened him, and he let rip with his mental defence thing. We think you might be able to contact him – from a distance, and arrange peace talks – or something.'

'How far does this mental wave thing reach out?' asked Zuki.

'We're not sure, but in the early days a shuttle from one of our ships got within about two hundred kilometres of his place before the crew hightailed it out of there, and they refused point blank to go back.'

'You think, if we can get him to co-operate, he may be able to give the aliens a dose of whatever he does with his mind?' Zuki suggested, 'How do you know it will work on them?'

'We don't, but it works on any creature we put in his vicinity, so we think it's worth a try. The alternative is an all out war with normal weapons; we should win, but the cost would be enormous.'

'Put like that, I can't refuse,' Zuki replied reluctantly, 'what do you suggest I do?'

'We will send you out to the planet in one of our fastest ships. You will land in what we consider to be a safe area - that is somewhere far enough away from him, so as to not be affected, and then you can make your way towards his dwelling until you can pick up whatever he is radiating. From then on in, it's up to you to try and establish some form of communication with him. If things get too hairy, just pull out, and we will bring you home. You will have a comms unit so you can contact the orbiting ship, and they will relay it back to us. There are one or two other tests we would like to do first, and then we can ship you out.'

Zuki wondered if he would come out of this exercise alive, or at least with his mind intact.

The other tests took place the following day, but he couldn't understand what they were testing, and why – and they didn't tell him. Two days later, he was being ushered out to the shuttle, which would then take him up to the main ship for the outward bound journey to the planet, and a very uncertain future, as far as Zuki was concerned.

Twice they had to divert from their main course, as a warning was received that an alien ship had been picked up on their long-range sensors. Normally, they would have attacked it, but those in charge of such things thought it better not to be too aggressive until they had tried out the experiment with 'stinky'.

At last, 'stinky's' planet came into sight, and Zuki plus two others boarded the shuttle which would take them down to the surface.

'Not a lot of vegetation down there,' commented the pilot, 'at least not where we are landing. Which is just as well - some of the planet is thick jungle and you'd have a hell of a job hacking through it.'

The shuttle settled down in a cloud of dust, and when it had cleared, the ramp was lowered and Zuki's supplies plus a small land Rover were unloaded.

'Don't forget,' said the pilot, 'you can get in touch with us if things go wrong and you want out. We will be back in orbit, it won't take long to reach you, but don't get in contact unless you really need to. We don't want to alert our friend down here that something is going on.'

With that, Zuki stepped back from the craft, covered his eyes to protect them from the dust as the shuttle took off, and then it was gone. He was now alone on an alien world with no instruction manual, and a seemingly impossible task ahead of him.

Looking around, he could see almost barren ground, with a few small stumpy bushes trying to get a foothold among the smaller stones, the odd tuft of what looked like some sort of grass – and not much else. He had a small navigation finder which showed him where 'stinky's' dwelling was, where he was, and a couple of deep ravines or rift valleys between them. So far, he couldn't pick up any mental 'smells', or anything else, for that matter.

A light chill wind began to blow as the sun went down, and Zuki sought refuge in the Rover, the landing crew having thoughtfully loaded his supplies into every available space, not leaving him much room except in the driving seat. After a small meal, he settled down for the night, not expecting to get much sleep in his seat, but awoke early having slept quite well, and feeling refreshed.

The sun broke through the haze on the horizon, exaggerating the starkness of the gaunt landscape with long shadows. A hot drink and an energy bar brought him back to reality, and he started the engine of the Rover. He wondered why he had not been issued one of the hover type craft, as the Rover rattled and clanked over the rough ground, and then realised it would have been too big to get into the shuttle – and perhaps there was not enough time to make a smaller version.

As the sun rose higher in the sky, the air warmed up, and it wasn't long before he was sweating in the small confines of the driver's cabin. A quick look around the controls to see if there was some sort of air conditioning available proved negative. If he didn't do something, he thought he would cook in his own juices by midday.

Zuki stopped the Rover. Perhaps he could open the access door to let in a little air? He tried this, but the Rover's engine wouldn't start with the door open. Some sort of safety device, he concluded, in case he got thrown out on rough terrain. The thought of that sent a shiver down his back as he visualised the Rover racing ahead, and him not being able to catch up with it.

To one side of the controls was a small lever. It didn't indicate what it was for, so he gently eased it forward, ready to wrench it back again if anything untoward happened, and then the transparent shield in front of him swung upwards, allowing in a gush of warm air. Zuki slammed the access door shut and hit the power button. He was underway again.

The rougher ground gave way to coarse sand interspersed with rock piles after a few minutes, and he was grateful for the smoother ride, although it did twist and turn rather a lot. But the navigation unit kept him in the right general direction.

Reaching the top of a rise in the terrain, he could see a formidable range of jagged rocks ahead, with a gully leading down into an area which seemed to be shrouded in mist. The navigation unit indicated that he should proceed down the gully – did it somehow know the correct way? Or did it merely point him in the general direction of 'stinky's dwelling? He looked about him – he couldn't see a way around the rock barrier, it seemed to stretch from side to side of the terrain. The only way open was down the gully.

Zuki gently eased the Rover down the slope and into the gap in the rocks with its misty patch up ahead. Soon the rock walls either side towered over him, and he had a feeling of being trapped. But he could always back out – but there was no rear-view window – he couldn't see to steer. The feeling of being trapped in the gully increased.

The mist patch ahead seemed to be alive, swirling about with a life of its own – but there was no wind down here – so what the hell was it? He soon found out, as the first of the flying insects entered the control cabin, and buzzed about angrily. Instinctively he tried to swat it, but it dodged his hand and landed on his other arm, sinking its stinger deep into his flesh. Without thinking, he flattened it with one mighty swipe, leaving a deep blue stain on his arm – blue? What did this thing use for blood?

Luckily for Zuki, as soon as his hand came off the controls, the Rover automatically stopped, otherwise it would have crashed into the rock wall of the gully. Instinctively, he pulled the lever to shut the viewing shield. The sting in his arm hurt with a burning fury, and he tried to squeeze the poison out, but with little success. Slowly his vision blurred, and then faded out all together – there was only a peaceful blackness as his body tried to neutralise the poison and repair the damaged tissue.

That which had changed his mind so long ago, also altered some of his body's abilities, and now it was building an anti venom to combat any further stings he might get in the future.

When Zuki's eyes opened, it was night-time, and the stars lit the gully with a pale ethereal light. Of the swarming clouds of stinging insects there was no sign, and he heaved a sigh of relief for that. The swelling on his arm had gone down, and he was feeling reasonably well – but it was too dark to risk using the Rover, although it was fitted with basic lights.

He opened the front viewing shield and let in the cool night air, talking a few deep breaths. It was then that he noticed the sweet honey smell he knew so well back in his village. In those days, they would follow the smell to locate the beehive, and take a little honey, always leaving enough for the bees to survive on through the cold months of winter. Was there honey here? He would follow the smell; a little honey would augment his more mundane food supplies.

Leaving the Rover, he looked around for any sign of the dreaded flying creatures, but there were none to be seen. The smell of honey grew stronger as he walked along the gully, and then he found its source. Several huge blue flowers, nearly a metre across, hung down from big vines which were clinging to the rocky walls, their stems almost as thick as his arm. He drew close to one of the flowers and took a deep sniff – the smell was almost overpowering, and his head swam for a moment.

So there was no honey, just the smell emitted from the flowers, but to what purpose? Everything had a purpose in nature, but this one evaded him for the moment. He sensed there was danger here. It was when he was on his way back to the Rover, and the first streaks of light in the sky heralded the coming dawn, that the reason for the flowers was revealed.

As he approached the Rover, several caterpillar-like creatures wriggled along the gully floor, heading for the area where the flowers bloomed. From above, a small group of flying things were circling around, getting lower all the time. They looked a bit like the birds he knew from long ago, but these were bigger with strange shaped wings, and a dull grey in colour.

Slowly they lost height, and then the first one hovered in front of one of the huge blue flowers, almost disappearing in the bell-like structure. It backed out on fluttering wings, its beak dripping a pale blue liquid and slowly sank to the ground. The wings twitched a few more times, but with little effort – and then stopped. Another bird entered the flower, only to join the other on the ground a few moments later. Zuki stood there fascinated as the small flock of flying creatures gradually diminished, until they were all lying prone on the gully floor.

The caterpillar creatures had by now reached the base of the vines, and began to climb – they too would soon join the other creatures below. Zuki sensed that something else was about to happen, so he ran to the Rover, climbed inside and slammed the door shut, just as the first of the stinging creatures took to the cool morning air to find their first meal of the new day, and then realised just in time that the viewing port was still open, and closed it just as one of the flying stingers approached.

Soon, a cloud of stingers filled the bottom of the gully, giving the impression of a moving cloud of mist. Zuki had seen enough, and gunned the Rover into action, how many stingers he squashed as they fed on the doped creatures on the gully floor he knew not as the Rover made its way out of the nightmarish scene, and into a clear glade with a pool of water in its middle.

The rocky walls still towered above him, but they were adorned in a multitude of flowering bushes and clumps of a grassy growth. It looked too quiet and peaceful to be true, so he looked around for the hidden dangers it might contain – but there was nothing, not even an insect could be seen. He was tempted to open the forward viewing screen to let the fresh air in, but as the heat of the day hadn't built up yet, he thought it might be wiser to keep it closed until he had left this strange place.

A few more twists and turns, and he was out of the gully and into the open, finding he was at the bottom of one of the rifts he had seen on the navigator screen. All around the steep sided cliffs were a barrier, so where did he go now? The navigator screen indicated he go towards the highest part of the cliffs, but there was no sign of another gully to go up – which didn't make much sense. Zuki turned the Rover towards the other end of the rift, where the side walls of rock seemed much lower, perhaps there was a way out there.

He had gone barely a few metres when a persistent beeping began. He looked at the navigator screen. A red bar was blocking his way on the screen, while the direction arrow still pointed towards the high part of the encircling cliffs. Zuki didn't like the idea that a mere machine could overrule his decisions, but the continuous beeping was beginning to get to him, it seemed the only way to stop it was to turn around and follow the arrow, so he did.

As the cliff face loomed up, he noticed a dark opening he hadn't seen before. Maybe there was a way out, but he didn't like what he saw – it had a dark foreboding look about it – it wasn't just dark, it seemed to suck the light around it into the opening. Making sure the viewing screen was firmly closed, he edged the Rover into the opening, and switched on the forward lights. The dark walls of the tunnel glistened in the headlights, as though they were wet, but the floor of the upward sloping tunnel showed no sign of moisture.

There were a few bends in the passage, as though whatever had made it had encountered a particularly hard bit of rock, and had gone around it. As the steepness increased, and the power unit dropped a gear to compensate, slowing down its progress, that uneasy feeling swept through Zuki again.

The vehicle turned a slight bend, and he saw his way was barred by what looked like a thick curtain of ropes, hanging down from the roof of the tunnel. They were moving slightly, as if a gentle wind was disturbing them, and before he could stop the Rover, it had hit the first of the dangling tendrils. A soft squishy sound accompanied their bursting as they contacted the Rover, and the screen was splashed in the slimy juice they contained. Zuki thought he heard a faint screech as the Rover ploughed on through the hanging curtain – and then he was through, and out into the open tunnel with its jet-black menacing walls.

A few more twists and turns, and he was out of the tunnel and on the open plateau. The scenery was now a little different, the occasional tall tree reached up into the sky – at an unbelievable height. Zuki wondered how such a tall tree could possibly withstand any wind, and a soft wind was blowing. He could just about make out the greenery at the top of one tree, and it seemed to flutter in the breeze, but no other part of the huge structure moved.

Apart from the trees, small bushes were dotted about between them, but still leaving plenty of space for him the drive between. A sort of grass covered the surface of the ground, but it wasn't like the grass of home – this was a closely packed mat of tiny curls, a mere couple of centimetres high, and soft and springy when he stopped the Rover to stretch his legs.

This was a pleasant world, he thought, warm despite its distance from its parent sun, nice grass to walk on, why move on? Just in time he realised something was touching his mind, and altering his thoughts – he quickly got back into the Rover and powered it up.

He had been travelling unhindered by any other anomalies the planet had to offer towards his destination, when he noticed the sun dip below the horizon. Zuki stopped the Rover, and wondered about spending the night under the stars instead of the cramped conditions inside his transport – and then thought better of it. Who knows what might roam about in the hours of darkness?

Zuki watched the stars come out as he ate his frugal meal, mainly based on concentrates, had a hot drink, and settled down for the night. During the night, something large and heavy prowled around the Rover, leaving deep footprints in the curly grass, but by morning the grass had recovered, and the signs of his visitor had disappeared.

It took two days of difficult, but unthreatening travel to come to the next rip in the planet's surface. A deep ravine stretched across the land, but the navigator still pointed to the land across the gap. Zuki stopped the Rover and got out, walking up to its edge. He looked down, and wished he hadn't – it was a sheer drop of some hundred meters to the valley below, and as far as he could see, there was no way down for him or the Rover.

Once he had got over the feeling of frustration which had swept over him, he tried to apply a little logic. The navigator pointed to the ravine's edge, so the direction must be right, it was just a matter of working out how to get down.

In desperation, he lay down and crawled to the edge to peer over, and discovered he was on an overhang. Below him he could see a narrow path, snaking its way along the rock face to eventually reach the valley bottom – but where did it start? If he could find that, he might just stand a chance.

He got to his feet, and walked along for some hundred metres or so, and crawled to the edge again. The path was still there, but now it was much nearer the top of the ravine. He was nearly out of sight of the Rover before he found the beginning of the way down, tucked away behind a rocky outcrop. It looked just wide enough for the Rover, if he was very careful, but it was very risky.

It was long walk back to the Rover, and he sank into the driving seat with a sigh of relief. Turning the Rover towards the distant rocky outcrop, he half expected the red 'no go' bar to reappear blocking his progress, but it didn't. The beginning of the downwards track was wider than he had first thought, and as the Rover tipped forward to begin its descent, he felt almost happy with his lot – he had survived the alien life the planet had to offer, and had now solved the problem of the huge rift which had so far prevented him from completing his mission.

By the time he was a quarter of the way to the valley floor, a dark opening unexpectedly appeared in the sheer wall of the rift, and there seemed to be a light deep within it. It was only a gentle glow, but it shouldn't be there. He stopped the Rover, making sure it was firmly positioned with its front almost touching the rock wall – if he lost it now, his days would be numbered, and there wouldn't be many of them.

The hole in the rift wall was arched with a flat floor, and knowing such things do not happen in nature, he was being extra cautious as he approached the glow, in case it was a trap of some kind. Six metres from the light he could see what it was, just a big blob of a jelly-like substance, softly glowing in its dark cave. But what was it? He felt tempted to poke it with a finger, but restrained himself just in time. A flying insect, the first he had seen for some time, buzzed past him to alight on the blob, it seemed to give way a little at the point of contact, and then envelope the creature in a lip-like structure of its own material, the insect disappeared from view.

Zuki concluded that things on this world had a very strange way of obtaining their nourishment, and were best left alone – but he did feel the unconscious desire to touch it, and that could be a bit worrying, if he couldn't override it.

Back in the Rover, he backed it away from the wall, and continued his journey down the narrow path to the valley bottom. The base of the rift was composed of sand and small stones, with the odd boulder which had fallen from the cliffs above at some time in the past. His next problem was to find a way out of the valley, and up onto the plateau above. There were no dark holes in the valley walls that he could see, so where was the exit? It had to be here somewhere, as the navigator had guided him to this place, and so far, it had never been wrong.

Zuki spent the rest of the day searching for the exit, but could not find it. He gave up as night began to fall, thinking a rest and a fresh look in the morning may reveal it. The night seemed to drag on forever, interspersed with dreams of being trapped in different situations, and he was glad of the first sign of dawn breaking – and that was his saviour.

Due to the angle of light in the valley, the path out was concealed from view, but now as the first beams of sunlight hit the wall opposite him, he could just about make it out – another narrow path leading up to the rim of the rift, but first he must find its beginning on the valley floor. Tracing the path down from the dizzy heights of the rim was difficult, as the rock all looked the same, but the slanting light of dawn illuminated its edge, and he hastened over to it just to make sure it was real.

A quick meal and a drink, and he was on his way up towards the top of the rift, one or two places needing very careful navigation as the path narrowed, probably due to past rock falls. But who had made this path? Could it possibly be a freak work of nature? He didn't think so, but he had no way of finding out.

Reaching the top of the cliffs, Zuki stopped the Rover, and got out. He was soaked in sweat, and trembling, and only then realised just how dangerous the journey up had been. He gave a sigh of relief as he remembered the map didn't show any other rifts in the planets surface, at least not on the journey marked out for him.

As he was standing there, he sensed something in his mind, something washed over him, making him shudder. Was this 'stinky' radiating his feelings about the probable invasion of his solitude? Zuki didn't think so, as nothing had happened to warn 'stinky' as far as he knew.

He climbed back into the Rover, checked the direction was correct with the navigator, and started the engine. After a while the terrain changed, the flat plateau acquired a few small rises and dips which gradually developed into full blown hills, with clumps of large trees adorning their tops. He checked the navigator and found he was only about eighty kilometres from 'stinky's' dwelling – and so far, he hadn't received a mental warning blast. According to what he had heard, the aliens had been sent packing at two hundred kilometres.

Zuki got to thinking as to what he would do when he got closer to his target, and 'stinky' didn't like it. Would he be able to withstand the mental thump others had received? And then he remembered something he had read in one of the physics books at the Academy. No two identical things can exist in the same space and at same time, and if they are forced to do so, they cancel each other out. It seemed to make sense, but how could he do it? Maybe if when he received the first pulse of mental thought from 'stinky', he accepted it, and tried to duplicate it – mentally make a copy of what he received – he didn't know if he would be able to, but it seemed the only available option.

Zuki stopped the Rover – he needed to concentrate. First, he would have to chose something he didn't like, something which was a threat to him – the 'stingers' from the first valley he had gone down. He imagined a stinger in front of him – he could see it clearly, and as he looked at it in detail, it vanished – he couldn't hold the picture in his mind. He tried again, but this time the stinger picture was slightly different – again, as he took in all the detail he could, and it too vanished. It seemed to work, but would it work with 'stinky' if he got really upset at the invasion of his privacy?

Zuki knew his abilities had been enhanced by the event with the crystal so long ago, but would they be enough to keep him safe from what 'stinky' could do with his mind?

The Rover trundled on, eating up the kilometres effortlessly, and Zuki began to wonder about the sequence of events which had led up to the alien's hasty withdrawal.

Maybe they had radiated out mental aggressive thoughts about what they were going to do, 'stinky' picked it up, and reacted. He would have to clear his mind of everything except just being a benign friendly being – and see what happened.

How the hell had he got himself into this frightening mess? Life used to be so pleasant and simple – but that was a long time ago.

His first warning that he was getting close to his target came the following day. Something brushed across his mind – it was almost like a foul smell – he accepted it, duplicated it - and it was gone. The Rover climbed up to the top of the hill, and he was looking down on a small hut in a clearing among some trees. Was this it? He stopped the Rover, and got out, his thinking being that if he casually approached on foot, it would be the least threatening way of making contact. At that moment, a small figure came out of the hut, turned in his direction, and stopped.

The first pulse of thought took Zuki by surprise – it was an overwhelming stink of something long dead, and rotting – he duplicated it, and it was no more. Zuki raised a hand and waved, calling out 'Hello' as he slowly walked towards the lone figure before him. Another pulse of something disgustingly awful – he handled it, and kept on walking. When he was about ten metres from the man, he stopped and smiled.

'Who the hell are you?' the figure called out, 'and what are you doing here?'

'I came here to explore this world – I didn't know anyone else was here, my apologies for intruding upon your space. Is it alright for me to come closer?'

'Suppose so,' the figure replied hesitatingly, 'how come you are not affected by my mental smell? Everyone else is.'

'I hadn't noticed anything,' Zuki lied, 'all I can smell are the flowers over there, they are very pleasant indeed. Anyway, what do I call you? My name is Zuki.'

'I've been called any number of names, most of them insulting. If I remember right, my name is Kono, or something like that. It's been a very long time since I spoke to a human, or anything else for that matter. What's that thing up on the hill?'

'Oh, that's my transport,' Zuki replied smiling, 'it enables me to cover large distances without walking, and also provides somewhere safe to sleep at night. You have some very strange creatures here, and some of them are not very friendly.'

'I don't see many, and most of them run away when I do,' Kono said, 'I don't understand how you can be so close and not be affected.' He added thoughtfully.

'If I make you feel uncomfortable, I can go away,' said Zuki, trying to make Kono feel more at ease, 'there is still a lot of this world to explore.'

'There's no need to,' Kono replied, 'it's nice to be able to talk to someone after all this time.'

'You mean no one comes to visit you?' Zuki responded, trying to sound sorrowful, 'why would that be?'

'That's a long story,' Kono said, 'and I'm reluctant to tell it, as it seems so impossible to most people. Anyway, do you want something to eat or drink?'

Zuki couldn't believe his luck – the man seemed friendly enough, so what was all the fuss about? And then he remembered the first mental shock he had received as he approached the dwelling.

'I could certainly do with something to drink,' Zuki said, 'my water supply is getting a bit stale.'

Kono turned, and beckoned Zuki towards the hut. By the time they had reached it, they were walking side by side, and Zuki felt nothing untoward.

'Sit down,' said Kono, 'I'll get you some fruit juice, the food isn't up to much, but you are welcome to it if you are hungry.'

The pair sat down at a crude table, clinked drinking mugs, and drank their fill.

'How do you get on for food?' asked Zuki, realising he would have to gently ease into the story of the castaway, and so not induce any stress.

'They send down a supply every now and again, when they think I need it.' He replied.

'So, who are they?' asked Zuki, innocently.

'The sods who dumped me here. I'm hated by my fellow men, they can't stand my company, and it's not my fault.' Zuki got a mental whiff of something very unpleasant, and handled it quickly.

'I would be interested to hear your story, that's if you would like to tell it,' Zuki said.

'It's a long story,' Kono replied, 'so you'd better have something to eat first.'

A tin was produced, and a pile of flat biscuit like objects were tipped out onto a plate.

'They are supposed to contain all the vitamins and minerals I need, plus protein, I suppose they work, I haven't died yet,' Kono said gloomily.

Zuki bit into one, and was pleasantly surprised.

'They taste rather good, better than those I have in the transport,' he said, 'I'd be pleased to swap supplies any time you like,' He added, trying to be as cheerful as possible, 'so how did you come to be here?'

'A long time ago our solar system was attacked by aliens – much to our surprise, we hadn't encountered any other life forms until then. They just came at us out of the blue, no warning, attacking our outer most planet without reason. We had a small space fleet, and managed to repel them, and by a stroke of luck captured one of them alive.' Kono paused for a moment, as if gathering the most salient points of the story.

'I had the job of debriefing the ugly little sod, but he wasn't giving anything away. I was told to use any methods necessary to find out all I could – no holds barred – and they weren't. I don't know exactly what happened, but there was a blinding flash of light, and I passed out for quite a long time. When I regained consciousness, I was told the alien had exploded, or something like that, making a terrible mess, and I had been in a coma.'

Kono paused to take a drink, and studied Zuki's face to see how he was taking it.

'After that, all hell broke loose. The aliens left the system and were never seen again, but I was in one hell of a mess. Nothing seemed real – it was as though I was in a permanent nightmare – I have never been so frightened in my life. So, I was told later, I was given some experimental drugs to try and stabilize me – and that's when the real trouble began.

Every time I felt stressed, and that was often, everyone ran screaming from the place. And it got worse with time. To shorten the story, they seemed to think when the alien blew its mind, it affected me in some way, and the new drugs just added to the problem. They shot me full of some sort of tranquilliser, and dumped me on this God forsaken planet. They apologised for what they had done, but explained that I gave out a mental stink which was a killer. They keep me supplied with most things I need, including food of a sort, but the worst thing is that there is no cure for my condition.'

Kono sat back in his chair, drained from the effort of going through what had happened to him.

'I think that's awful,' said Zuki, trying to sound sympathetic, 'are you sure there's nothing they can do?'

Kono just shook his head, resigned to his plight.

'I think that's terrible,' said Zuki, 'I'm sure something can be done to help you. When I get back to my home world, I'll make some enquiries – I know people with some influence.'

Kono didn't say anything, he just poured out some more drink, and then pushed the plate of biscuits towards Zuki.

'I don't feel threatened or frightened by you,' Zuki began again, 'you seem quite normal to me. I think I would have lost it if I'd been left here all on my own with no hope of meeting up with my fellow men. I am wondering if your unfortunate affliction couldn't be put to good use – I'll have a think about it.' A plan was already forming in Zuki's mind.

'I don't know of anyone who hasn't been affected by my presence,' Kono said, 'so how come you aren't?'

'I don't know,' Zuki lied.

They talked on for some time, mainly on things which wouldn't stimulate Kono's mind to send out a blast of destruction; and as the light began to fade, Kono suggested Zuki bring the transport down to the hut, and stay the night.

Zuki lay on a mattress stuffed with dried grass, and found it much more comfortable than the chair in the Rover, but he couldn't sleep, his mind was racing to find a way of getting Kono's co-operation to use his lethal mind bending affliction to fend off the new wave of aliens which threatened their planetary system.

Next morning, Zuki decided to play it safe, and not put too much pressure on Kono. He would have to get his complete trust before he dared mention the real reason for his visit. After a somewhat frugal breakfast, Kono offered to show Zuki some remains of what he thought were possible humanoid creatures he had found on one of his excursions.

Zuki realised it might have been the aliens which had earlier left in a hurry, abandoning their companions to their fate. They set off down a well trodden path towards the edge of the clearing in which the hut lay, Kono explaining that the next clearing held his vegetable patch, although not all the seeds he had requested germinated, but those which did gave him a varied diet.

'You seem to be very well organised,' said Zuki, thinking a little praise might be helpful, 'some of those would surely win prizes in a growing competition.' Although he didn't really recognise any of them.

The path wound down to a small river, and Zuki was about to wade in when Kono grabbed his arm, pulling him back to the bank.

'If you enter that water, it'll be the last thing you do,' Kono exclaimed, 'there are very few animals here, but I saw one a long time ago go down for a drink, and it disappeared below the surface as if something had dragged it in. I don't know what it was, as all I saw was the churned-up water and a fast-disappearing rear end of a four-legged creature. We will have to go down stream a little, and cross on some convenient rocks.'

The stepping stones were reached, and although the water was crystal clear and Zuki couldn't see anything in the water, he made sure each step was in the middle of each stone, and went across with indecent haste, much to Kono's amusement.

Just before the sun reached its zenith, they came across the remains of the aliens. Bits of what were once uniforms lay scattered about among some odd-looking bones; what few bones that were still attached to each other looked as if the bodies had torn themselves apart, Zuki commenting that there were no teeth marks on them, so it could not be put down to animals. Lying next to one group of bones lay a metallic looking object, and Kono bent down to pick it up.

'STOP.' yelled Zuki, 'I think I know what that might be, and it's deadly.' He had heard about the neutron grenade, a device the aliens had used to clear the old mining operation.

'I've never seen anything like that,' said Kono, 'is it something new?'

'Yes.' replied Zuki, hoping he wouldn't have to elaborate on the issue.

'But why would people try to come here when they know what would happen to them?' asked Kono, puzzled.

Zuki saw his chance, but he would have to be very careful.

'Just take a look at those bones,' he said, 'do they look human to you?'

'Come to think of it, no,' Kono said, looking even more puzzled, 'you mean they are alien?'

'I would think so, they're certainly not from our race.' Zuki replied, 'although two of our worlds are inhabited, the main body structure is much the same.'

'You mean they're from outside our system?' Kono seemed shocked, 'like the last lot where I got screwed up?'

'Yes, it's very recent,' said Zuki casually, wondering if he had said too much.

'Hmm,' said Kono, still thinking of the enormity of what that might imply.

The journey back to the shack was uneventful, and an evening meal with a few supplies from the Rover restored the atmosphere to some extent, but Zuki could see that something was still worrying Kono.

Next day, Kono suggested they have a look at some caves he had found, and the pair set off straight after their first meal of the day. Before long Kono brought up the subject of the aliens, and what Zuki thought might happen if they decided to invade.

'So far as I know, their weapons are not superior to ours, and as there are a lot more of us, we should win – but it would lead to an awful lot of destruction on our worlds.

I was wondering, do you think you could direct your killer thoughts towards a specific target? Or do they radiate out in all directions?'

'I don't know,' replied Kono, 'I've never tried to do that. It just seems to happen when I'm stressed – I don't mean to do it, it just happens, that's why they dumped me here, well away from everyone else.'

Zuki thought it might be the time to come clean, and tell Kono what his visit was all about, but just then the caves came into view, which, as it turned out, was very fortunate.

Chapter 3
A Repeat Performance

'I FOUND THESE not long after I got dumped here,' said Kono, 'but I've never explored them properly – I feel sort of drawn to them, but it's not a nice feeling when you are on your own.'

'Don't blame you, I wouldn't have either.' said Zuki, meaning every word.

It was just a dark hole in a massive cliff face, and not very inviting, but Kono walked in as if he owned the place.

'We can only go in a short distance,' he said, 'as it's black as pitch further in, and I pick up a strange feeling in here.'

Something about the cave reminded Zuki of something, but he couldn't quite recall what it was for the moment.

'We could make a torch from brushwood,' he offered, 'that should take us in a bit further.'

They made three torches, lit one, and entered the cave again. Some twenty metres in, Kono stopped.

'There's an odd feeling in here, do you sense it?'

'Yes,' Zuki replied, remembering the cave back on his home world – if he was right, did he dare do what he was thinking?

'Let's go in a little further,' Zuki said, 'I think I know what it's all about, but I want to be sure first.'

Another ten metres in, and he was sure. In the distance, a faint glow could be seen, and the torch light seemed to be sucked towards it.

'You don't have to do this – so think about it carefully. Back in my home world, I found a cave like this, went in, and saw a glow like that up ahead. I too, had a torch, and as I got closer to the light, it seemed to suck in the light from my torch and the crystal glowed brighter– and then I had the unstoppable urge to touch the crystal – I couldn't stop myself.

There was a blinding flash of light, and when I woke up, I knew I was different – something about me had changed. Later I found I could learn things much faster that others, and I had a lot of other skills as well. I can't really explain it, but it seems as if the crystal held some sort of life form trapped inside it, and rather than stay there, it joined me – somehow. You don't have to do this, but if it works the same as it did for me, you will have greatly enhanced abilities, much more than you can imagine.'

'So that's why you are different,' said Kono 'I knew there was something, you are not like other men.'

'So, what are you going to do?' asked Zuki firmly, 'you have two choices, touch the crystal, or spend the rest of your life wondering what it would have been like if you had done so.'

Kono passed his torch to Zuki, gave him one hard look in the flickering light, and stepped forward. The flash of light even took Zuki by surprise, and after a few moments to let his eyes return to normal, lit the next torch, and then dragged the unconscious body of Kono out of the cave and into daylight.

Had he done the correct thing? Only time would tell if he had got it right, and the prone body of Kono gave no clue.

The light began to fail as Kono came out of his unconscious state; he looked around, saw Zuki, and pointed a finger at him.

'You crafty sod,' he said, 'you knew all along what would happen, so now there are two of us – God help the world if anyone upsets us now!'

'Seriously though, how do you feel?' asked Zuki, 'do you notice any changes,'

'I feel very alert,' Kono replied, 'almost powerful – it's a strange feeling.'

'With enhanced abilities,' said Zuki seriously, 'comes increased responsibilities, you must use your new powers with restraint and care – I have learnt a lot over the last few years, and I will help you to do the same. Your first task will be to control that mind blast of yours.'

Kono shook his head several times, as if doing so would return things back to normal, but it didn't.

The pair made their way back to the hut as the first few stars came out – somehow, they seemed to be that little bit brighter.

After a meal, they sat discussing what had happened and its implications well into the night, but the significance of the strange crystal and the full story behind it which had affected them both, would remain a mystery for a little longer.

Next day, after explaining to Kono what would happen, Zuki contacted the orbiting ship, and the shuttle came down. The shuttle crew were advised to land a good two hundred kilometres away from the hut site, and then approach it in fifty-kilometre stages just to see if Kono had full control of his ability to blast minds apart.

Zuki knew all was well when one of the crew appeared at the top of the rise leading down to the hut, and beckoned him on. Introductions were made, the crew members still a little hesitant, but that disappeared after a while when a few jokes had been exchanged.

'You know, I shall miss my home here, strange as it may seem,' said Kono, 'I've been here a very long time, and grown used to the place.' The others nodded, there was little they could or dare say, on that subject.

As Kono was about to enter the shuttle, he turned, with one more wistful look at his old home, and then stepped aboard – he was about to begin a new stage in his life – and so was everyone else.

Kono was a little apprehensive about space travel as he had only experienced it once, and then he was under heavy sedation. The fear among the crew was that he would get stressed, and cook their minds, but it didn't happen; they arrived at the orbiting transfer station, boarded a shuttle, and landed on Zuki's home world with a communal sigh of relief.

In his absence, the top brass had at long last realised that Zuki had abilities they didn't – and in spades. It was decided to give him full control of the experiment to test out Kono's abilities against the aliens, especially as more of their ships had been detected on the fringes of their planetary system – were they getting ready for a full-scale invasion? And then came the news that the other smaller mining operation on the other side of the mining planet had been wiped out – or at least they weren't getting any signals from it. No one had thought to evacuate them in the general panic.

The main problem was keeping the whole exercise secret until they had a positive result – as there was no point in panicking the general populous unnecessarily.

When the news of his new exalted position was broken to Zuki, he was a little surprised, but also relieved. Some of the big wigs gave the impression that they were not too sure what day of the week it was on occasions, and this exercise would have to go faultlessly if the enemy were not to be forwarned of what they could expect; that's if it worked.

A spaceship with the latest long range detectors and a powerful laser canon was on standby, all that was needed was a strategy for how to test out Kono's new refined ability. There was little point in rushing out and blasting everything in sight, as this would alert the aliens to the fact that they had been detected - something the home team had sensibly kept quiet about.

The crew consisting of a pilot, navigator, weapons man, and an engineer to handle any faults which may arise, and of course, Kono and Zuki, who suggested that they go out to the old mining planet where the second lot of workers had been eliminated by the aliens, and see if an alien ship was still in the vicinity.

The shuttle journey up to the waiting attack ship was uneventful, except that Kono looked a bit apprehensive until they had reached their destination, and then he seemed to calm down. They transferred to the attack ship and took up their positions, and then the long journey out began.

The detectors were of a new type, sending out random pulses of very short duration, such that if they were picked up, they could be mistaken for random space noise, and hopefully ignored.

The crew were getting a bit tense by the time they located the mining planet, especially Kono, who had nothing to do except sit there, while Zuki ran through in his mind every possible scenario he could think of, and what actions to take.

'The aliens have been assembling on the outer fringes of our system,' said Zuki, 'or so I have been informed. If we stay behind the mining planet and occasionally slip out to one side and do a sweep with the detectors, we should pick up anything approaching us; then it's just a matter of slipping around the planet to keep out of sight, and see what they are up to. Once they have landed, Kono can go to work.'

'What makes you think they will return? asked the pilot, 'they've wiped out the workers like the first lot, why would they come back?'

'I assume an attack ship was used to kill our men,' Zuki responded, 'and that would not normally have the means to land on the planet. I think they will return, with a landing shuttle to see what we were mining, and to gather any other information about us that they can – that's what I would do in their circumstances.'

Two days of ship time passed before the detectors registered an in coming object, and the tension mounted as the possible confrontation with the aliens drew nearer, with Kono looking particularly worried.

On board they had a small drone, which using the latest deflection technology, should be able to spy on any activity taking place on the planet's surface without being seen, and to that end, it was sent down to land near the old workings.

'I've got a reflection signal from that object, and it's not one of ours,' the navigator announced, 'and it's heading this way – time we moved out of sight.'

The ship edged around the planet, just out of sight of the mining complex, and they waited to see what would happen next. Time dragged by, and then the alien ship took up a geostationary orbit, and a tiny blip on the screen showed the launching of their shuttle.

'OK navigator, give 'em time to land,' said Zuki, 'and then bring the drone into range. I want to see just what they are up to.'

The drone lifted off, and flew a few centimetres above the surface of the planet until they had a clear picture of the aliens and their shuttle.

'Two of the aliens are dragging one of our men towards the shuttle,' said the navigator, 'and it looks as if they are going to take it on board – yes, they have. And now they are bringing in another one.'

'Right,' said Zuki, 'Kono, see if you can take out those left on the orbiting ship, and then we'll attend to the ones on the surface.'

Kono had felt a surge of anger as he heard about the aliens roughly handling the dead mine workers, and the crew all felt something radiating from their secret weapon, but no one was sick – yet.

He looked out of the viewing port as the ship slowly moved around to bring the alien ship into sight, concentrated all his attention on the ship, and then they all shuddered as he sent out the first pulse from his altered mind.

'How do we know if it has worked,' asked the pilot, 'we can't see into their ship.'

'Good point,' Zuki replied, 'bring us around and a bit closer, if they are still alive, they'll swing around to bring their weaponry in line with us – if the ship moves, Kono, give 'em another couple of blasts.'

The alien ship hung there in space without moving – Kono had succeeded, as far as they could tell.

'Move around them a bit more,' said Zuki, 'we want to be sure they are unable to respond.'

The alien ship stayed where it was, with no sign of movement, and the pilot moved their ship in close to the alien craft.

'If we stay close,' said the pilot, 'and the aliens are monitoring their obiter, they'll only see one signal, and not us.'

'Good thinking,' Zuki said, 'well done, I hadn't thought of that.'

After the aliens had loaded the two dead mine workers into their shuttle, they then collected another four, and unceremoniously dumped them down next to their vehicle, before going into the mine buildings.

'Move the drone a bit closer to the building when the last one is inside,' Zuki said, 'I want to see what they are doing.'

Unfortunately, the building had an airlock type entrance, and as it shut, the drone was left outside.

'OK,' Zuki ordered, 'move the drone to one side of the entrance so we get a good view of them when they come out and return to the shuttle, that's when Kono can zap 'em – OK Kono?' Kono nodded, his anger was still bubbling up, and the next pulse would be a big one.

After what seemed an age, the airlock door opened, and the two aliens emerged dragging a large box between them. When they were about halfway to the shuttle-

'OK, Kono,' Zuki said in a hard voice, 'let 'em have it – now.'

The two figures seemed to jerk about like puppets on a badly managed set of strings before falling to the ground and writhing about in what appeared to be extreme agony.

When, what they assumed to be alien blood began to appear, the crew turned as one to look away as the alien bodies tore themselves to pieces.

'I don't understand that,' said a shocked navigator, 'their space suits have ruptured, and space suits are as tough as hell – how did that happen?'

'I don't have all the data on how Kono does his thing,' Zuki replied, 'but it would seem that he sends out a wave of something which induces a feeling of utter nausea causing the body to vomit – and I don't mean just being sick – the poor sods on the receiving end bring up everything, and then follow with their internal organs. I've actually seen bodies which have torn themselves apart as the nervous system loses all control, and the muscles go into hyper drive, the nervous system being triggered randomly and literally ripping the bodies apart – you really don't want to witness it.'

'Do you want to take the shuttle down to have a look around?' asked the pilot quietly, hoping Zuki didn't hear him.

'I suppose we'd better do that,' Zuki replied, 'I'd like to see what they were mining, and if the aliens left any weapons behind.'

The shuttle slipped away from their ship with Zuki and the pilot aboard, neither of which were looking forward to what they would see up close. The shuttle landed near the box of minerals, and Zuki carefully extracted a small sample in a specimen bag, before turning his attention to the twisted remains of the aliens.

'If they could see this,' Zuki said, 'they would leave us in peace, but I doubt there is much chance of them doing that, or even understand the enormity of what will happen to them if they persist in their aggression.'

The pair returned to their main ship to decide what they would do next, not that there was much they could do, except return to base.

Back on his home world, Zuki was called into the inner sanctum of the space research station to relate what had happened. Several of the gold braid encrusted higher members of those in charge of things military, looked several shades paler after Zuki recounted their venture on the old mining planet in full detail – he had to face it, and he thought they should too.

After much discussion, it was decided that Kono would be sent out to face the aliens, and see what they thought of what he had to offer. Zuki promptly put a stop to that.

'If they see us coming, they'll just blast us into oblivion,' he stated firmly, 'a little subtlety is need here. Sure, we'll use Kono, if he's in agreement, but we have to protect him – he's a massive asset, and we can't afford to lose him. Leave this with me for a while, and I'll come up with a safer method of operation.'

'We don't have the time to mess around,' said one of the chiefs haughtily, 'we need to sort out these aliens quick time.'

'If you don't allow Kono and me to run this operation, you can do so using your normal weapons – and take responsibility for what happens.' And with that, Zuki got up to go.

Chapter 4
Full Command

'WAIT A MOMENT,' one of the other high rankers said, 'I think you have a good point there, Zuki. You know much more about the aliens than any of us, and what they are capable of. I think you should be in sole charge; just keep us informed of what you propose to do.'

With that the meeting broke up, all going their separate ways, Zuki seeking out Kono to explain an idea he was slowly forming.

'Let's go to the canteen,' he said, 'I think I've found a solution to the problem of hitting the aliens safely.' Kono looked a bit apprehensive.

Sitting in a corner well away from the few others present, Zuki outlined his idea.

'If we made the smallest possible space craft, and fitted it with deflection camouflage, we should be able to get close to an alien ship without being detected. Your ship would be remotely controlled from some distance away, so you don't have to do anything except give them a blast from your mind – what do you think?'

'Like all your theories, it sounds quite good,' Kono responded, 'but I don't fancy sitting in a tiny tin box all on my own, and someone else controlling where I go; is there any other way we could do it?'

'That depends on the range of your thought pulse,' said Zuki, 'in theory, I don't see why it should be restricted to a specific distance – but we don't know; and the other thing is that you need to get into some sort of angry or threatened state to initiate it in the first place.'

'Got one idea, but I don't think you'll like it,' said Kono, 'get one of those nasty little sods who wrecked your village, stick him in a capsule hitched up to something which will tell us if he is still alive, and I'll try and take him out from a distance.'

'I'm glad you're on our side,' said Zuki, 'it's nasty, but practical – don't know if the General Council will go along with it though.'

'What options do they have?' asked Kono, 'left to their normal firepower, they might win, but at what cost? We could just go ahead and not say anything to anyone.'

'What you suggest would involve quite a few people, how can we guarantee their silence? If it got out afterwards, when the threat had gone, we would be pillared,' Zuki replied, 'there must be another way.'

They sat there in silence for a while, both trying to find a solution to an almost unsolvable problem - but it had to be solved.

'OK,' said Zuki, 'you and I could dart and capture one of those who wrecked my old home. We keep him asleep until we are ready; in the meantime, we tell the Council we will be using an ordinary probe with some instruments on board to see what sort of range you can operate at. If they accept that, we load our 'sample' on board with enough necessities to keep him alive – and you do your thing. We would then have to destroy the probe afterwards, to remove the evidence of what we have done – could say you gave it such a blast, it just disintegrated.'

'Sounds feasible,' said Kono, 'are there any people on the Council with enough technical savvy to ask awkward questions?'

'Only one, that I know of,' Zuki replied, 'and I think I could keep him quiet if I had to.'

Kono just nodded his head.

Capturing their 'sample' proved less difficult than they thought it would be, and he was safely stowed away in a storage unit on the outskirts of town, with an intravenous drip to keep his fluids topped up.

Zuki located an ancient shuttle, had an old space drive unit fitted to it, and then installed a load of redundant electronic equipment to represent the 'electronic detector' Kono would try to zap. This left little space for their 'sample', but as it would be comatose, it didn't really matter. Getting it in, would be a little more troublesome.

On the day of the launch, Zuki turned up with a long box,

'Just some more instrumentation,' he called out cheerfully to the men in the hanger, 'give us a hand to get it in.'

Afterwards, Kono commented, 'You've got a bloody nerve to do that, with all those people around.'

Zuki just gave him a grin and said,

'If you do something with enough intention and no counter intention, it somehow gets done. Right, let's hitch up the life detection equipment to our 'sample', and we can get under way.'

The old shuttle struggled its way up into outer space, and Kono and Zuki followed in another, then transferring to their own craft. Zuki took remote control of the old shuttle, cut in the space drive, and it was on its way into the solar system, as a target.

'While it's in sight, it shouldn't be a problem,' Zuki said to Kono, 'let's see if you can still get it when it's too small to see. You'll have to pick it up on the scanner, and then visualise where it is in space. The life detector says he is still alive.'

They waited until the old shuttle was just on the edge of their detection scope, and then Zuki gave the word. For several minutes nothing happened, and he was about to accelerate to catch up the old shuttle to see why they hadn't succeeded, when the life detector bleeped – they had done it. 'Right,' said Zuki, 'as soon as we have a visual, I'll hit the destruct button, there shouldn't be enough left for anyone to figure out what we've done.' Kono was silent.

A few moments later, there was a bright flash up ahead, and they turned their ship around and headed back to the transfer station.

At the debriefing, Zuki just stated that they had successfully got a direct hit with Kono's 'mind blast' from a scope reading, the target being out of sight. Unfortunately, the target disintegrated, probably due to a fault in the space drive, as it was a very old one.

The round of applause was deafening, but the jubilation the pair should have felt was somewhat reduced, as they finally realised the enormity of what they had done to a fellow being…

Part 2
A New Force

Chapter 5
A Force Released

Zuki's parents welcomed him with open arms, but were slightly hesitant about Kono, having heard rumours of his affliction.

'Sorry I couldn't get here sooner,' Zuki said, 'things got into a bit of a rush. But we have two days before we have to go off again; Brond said he had let you know I was well.'

'Yes, he did, but it's not the same as seeing you,' his mother said, 'anyway I don't always believe some of the officials we've met – they're a funny lot. So, what can you tell us of your adventures?'

'Not much really,' replied Zuki, 'we still have the same problem, but we think we've found a way to handle it – with Kono's help.'

His parents' eyes turned towards Kono, who smiled back in return, not sure what to say.

'I suppose this means you will be going away again for an undisclosed period, as before,' said his father, 'not that we can do anything about it.' He added, sadly.

'Yes, we both will – we work together,' Zuki replied, 'what we have discovered is mind blowing, literally,' he grinned, realising how near the truth he was, 'but we can't tell you anything until we have solved the problem we have.'

The two days leave went all too quickly for all of them, and Zuki and Kono returned to the underground complex to meet up with Brond.

'Sorry we couldn't give you more leave, but the Council is on our backs, and then some,' Brond said cheerfully, 'and they want to know what we are going to do about the alien threat. We have been asked to meet up with them and give them our proposals.'

The following day, all three entered the Council Chambers, looked around at the glum faces, and reluctantly sat down at the long table. One of the military men stood up.

'I understand your experiment went very well, but we now have a huge conglomeration of aliens on the outskirts of our system, and I don't see how one man can handle that lot.'

'I understand,' Zuki replied, 'but let's get some exact information – how many alien ships are there, and exactly where are they positioned?'

'At the last count, there were about eighteen of them, in two groups,' the military man said, 'one lot of six is only just within long range detection, and the others are positioned in a tight group just a short distance from the mining planet, but neither group has moved for the last few days. I think our only chance is to go out there in force, and blast 'em. We may have some casualties, but I don't see what else we can do.' He sat down, his face grimly set.

'I think I may have a better way of handling them,' Zuki said, thinking on his feet, 'what I propose is that we send out one of our ships, but somewhat modified. It will be under remote control, and at the right moment, will disgorge about four decoys which will spread out to surround the main ship, we need them to think they outnumber us and so will be more inclined to attack. The decoys will be, in effect, reflective balloons, such that they will appear to be part of a fleet. Each balloon will have a small amount of gas to be released when they are in position, inflating them to full size. To the aliens it will appear as though they have just materialised out of thin air, or should I say, space.'

Before he could continue, the military man jumped to his feet,

'I really don't see how a bunch of balloons will be of any help.' he said derisively.

'I hadn't finished,' Zuki retorted hotly, 'the balloons will appear as an attacking fleet, and draw the aliens to engage. If we position ourselves carefully, shielded by the mining planet, we can pick them off, one by one as they pass.'

'It will only take a flick from a laser or a missile to deflate the balloons,' the military man almost shouted, 'and then what do we do?'

'If you would be kind enough to let me finish,' Zuki said patiently, 'the balloons will be constructed from a plastic with stretched polymer sensitivity – in other words, when it is stretched at full inflation, it will go ridged and will not deflate, giving the impression that the 'balloon ship' is indestructible – that should worry them somewhat. Anything hitting the 'balloon ship' will just pass straight through. In the meantime, we reduce the speed of the main ship such that the decoys carry on towards the aliens.'

'How can the decoys carry on towards the aliens? They don't have a drive unit in them,' the military said smugly.

'They don't need a drive unit.' Zuki retorted, 'they have forward momentum imparted from the main ship when it disgorged them.'

Several of the company turned and glared at the military man, who went red in the face and visibly clamped his mouth shut.

'That just leaves the other lot of aliens, out on the fringes of our system' said Zuki, 'and we will have to take them out so that they can't report back to their home world for reinforcements. I think it a bit odd that the main fleet of aliens is twice the number of those which are hanging back – something about that doesn't quite add up – I think we should send out a shielded probe to see exactly what we have there.'

'Your suggestion about the inflatable 'ghost' ships sounds just about feasible,' said Brond, standing up, 'but it will need very careful positioning of the main ship such that the aliens do not impact on any of our worlds - I assume they will just carry on in the same direction?'

'Yes,' replied Zuki, 'they will, and by the time the other lot realise what's happened, it will be too late to do anything about it. Our next problem is drawing the other lot into the same sort of trap, but until we know what they are exactly and will do next, we can't plan for it.'

With that, the meeting drew to a close, instructions being given to those who would organize the manufacture of the decoy balloons and the modification to one of their standard spaceships to carry them, along with the long range vision probe.

Back in the canteen, Zuki, Kono and Brond helped themselves from the self-service bar and sat down to plan the next move.

'If we position ourselves just right, we should be able to approach the alien fleet from the shadow of the mining planet, and remain undetected,' said Zuki, 'and then Kono can zap them as they pass the planet towards our bogus attack force. We shall have to position that very carefully, and once the decoys have been released, the main ship will have to slow down, reverse, and return to Base – we may need it again – for the other lot.'

'Sounds practical,' said Kono, 'I just hope I can get every one of 'em as they pass.'

'I think we should send out the vision probe as soon as possible,' Brond suggested, 'we need to know what the other six alien ships are capable of, and what to do if they join the fray.'

'I wonder why the eleven alien ships are just staying put near the mining planet,' Zuki offered up for comment, 'as far as we know, they haven't moved for days, so what are they up to?'

'That's anyone's guess,' said Brond glumly, 'don't suppose they're just taking a few days off for recreation – that's too much to hope for.'

'What about the alien ship near the mining planet which we crippled?' asked Kono, 'surely they'll notice it and investigate?'

'Not much we can do about that,' replied Brond, 'if we send a tug out to move it behind the planet so it's out of sight, they'll see us – just hope they think its waiting to join them, in whatever they do next.'

'Just thought of something else,' said Zuki, 'we will need a small camera probe to be positioned so that we can see the aliens while we remain in the shadow of the mining planet, that way Kono will have plenty of warning to get ready for his mind blast.'

'I'll see to it,' said Brond, 'in the meantime, you'd better work out the positioning of our decoy ship, so they miss our planet as they go by it- we don't want them getting through to our home world.'

Zuki just nodded.

Two days later, and the announcement came through that the decoy ship, complete with its decoys, was ready.

'How the hell could they have done that in so short a time?' asked Zuki.

'I think little pressure was applied in the right places,' responded Brond with a grin, 'a lot is at stake, so no one was pussy footing about, so I've heard. Oh, we also have your vision probe. They've made it as small as possible, so the aliens won't detect it – we hope.'

The three of them set off for the orbiting space station, and their ship; the decoy ship and its load of decoys having already been positioned according to Zuki's instructions, such that they would be just outside of the aliens detector range, or so they hoped.

Keeping in the shadow of the old mining planet, their ship went into stationery orbit, and the vision probe was sent out to see what the aliens were doing, apart from just staying put.

The eleven alien ships were hardly visible on the vision probe's relay signals, but the long-range detector section sent back clear spots of light, showing them to still be in the same position as before.

'Right, let's get the show on the road,' said Brond, 'someone has to make the first move.'

'OK,' Zuki replied, 'let's bring our decoy ship into range of their detectors, that should produce some reaction.'

The signals were sent back to Base, and the decoy ship began to move slowly towards the alien fleet. Nothing happened for quite a while, and then an excited yelp from Zuki brought the other two over to the viewing screen.

'There's only one alien ship in view – where the hell are the others?' he asked in a shocked voice. Brond stared intensely at the screen, and then said:

'I think I know – you won't believe this – the silly sods have lined up behind each other, probably to make us think there is only one of them. Now that's what I call very good luck, it'll make Kono's job a lot easier as they stream by, one at a time – he can't miss.'

On Zuki's command, the decoy ship released its balloon decoys, decelerated, and turned for home. The decoys suddenly appeared as bright pinpoints of light in a tight circle as they inflated, heading for the alien fleet.

As the aliens approached the old mining planet, the first flicker of laser fire left the lead ship, and passed harmlessly through the on coming balloons, and then the first of many missiles were released – with much the same effect.

'I wonder what they made of that,' commented Zuki, 'their missiles have just passed through the decoys, and not even exploded.'

'Stand by, Kono,' said Brond, 'the first of the aliens is approaching fast, and should pass us in a minute or so. Let's hope they are looking straight ahead, and not to one side, or they'll see us at this range.'

The tension was almost palpable in the tiny control cabin as the alien fleet drew near, and Kono took up his position at the viewing window.

As the first alien ship drew level with them, Kono let rip with his mind blast, but there was no visible effect they could see – time would tell if he had been successful if the alien ship continued on its present course instead of curving around to engage with the 'balloons' – and it didn't.

After the fifth ship had passed and continued on in their original course, Kono was looking decidedly haggard, and his face was soaked in sweat.

'You OK Kono?' Zuki asked anxiously, 'breathe deeply and slowly, it seems to be working, they've all gone on in a straight line.'

As the last of the eleven alien ships passed, it veered off slightly from its original course – the aliens had realised something was not quite right, and tried to take evasive action, but they didn't know from what. Kono's concentration lapsed for a second, and then he refocused to send out one more of that dreadful thought pulse.

The alien ship seemed to jerk about for a while, as if those at the controls were not too sure what they were doing, and then its course straightened out again, still veering away from the decoys.

'Reckon you got him,' said Brond with a sigh of relief, 'don't know if they are dead or just severely mentally bruised. I'll call up a couple of our ships to come in around the back of them – just to make sure.'

'That just leaves the other six out in the fringes of our system,' commented Zuki, 'they must have seen what happened, and wondered why – but as far as I can tell, they haven't moved.'

'I'll see if I can get any results from the long-range vision probe,' Brond said, 'the data should be in by now – Base will know.'

Some minutes later, the pictures from the probe showed up on the ship's screen, and they all stared in silence.

'Just what the hell are those weird looking things?' exclaimed Kono, the first to speak, 'they look a bit flimsy, apart from those blobs at the rear end.'

'I think I can make an educated guess,' Brond offered, 'it looks like two semi circular cradles stuck together with a platform above, and those blobs at the rear are probably the drive units. I think the aliens brought their attack ships fully fuelled up in those carriers, and then released them when needed – that way they wouldn't have to mess about refuelling when they reached their destination – makes sense to me.' He added as an after thought.

'Do you think they're armed?' asked Zuki, wondering how they could entice the aliens to come closer, and if they would fall into the same trap the others had done.

'Just a minute,' said Brond, magnifying one of the images, 'our probe must have got really close to get a picture like this, and they haven't attacked it. That means they didn't see it, or couldn't do anything about it if they had. I think we should send something a bit bigger out to them, and see what they do about that – I'll give the orders.'

The balloon decoys continued in the same direction imparted to them when they had left the main decoy ship, but one, having been caught in the gravity of the mining planet, slowly drifted down to shatter in a cloud of dust just below Zuki's ship. The alien ships which Kono had zapped were now out of range of his ship's detectors, so all thoughts were now being focused on the six carriers – and what to do about them.

A while later, a message came up from Base to inform them that a small number of our attack ships would be sent to destroy the carriers, but Brond countered this, saying that he thought they could be captured, and therefore information about the aliens could be obtained – one way or another.

The unmanned remote-controlled decoy balloon ship was sent out at full speed to view the alien carriers, and the pictures sent back clearly indicated that the aliens, for one reason or another, didn't fire a single shot at it. It was therefore decided that the alien carrier ships were unarmed, and Brond was given the go ahead to pay them a visit – another attack ship being sent to accompany him – just in case.

As they approached the alien carriers, one broke rank and veered off to one side – a missile from Brond's accompanying attack ship prevented any further movement of the aliens as the 'run away' disintegrated in a bright flash as the drive units received a direct hit.

'Kono, can you reduce your mind blast to a level where the recipient is just knocked out?' asked Zuki, 'that way we could capture them and find out just what they're up to and why.'

'I'll try it on one of you, if you like,' Kono responded, with a grin, 'just a gentle little pulse – I think I can do that.'

'You think you can?' Brond said, 'not on me, you won't!'

'OK, seriously though, I noticed on that last alien ship I zapped, my concentration slipped a bit, and their control of the ship went all over the place before I finally got 'em. I'll be really careful, if one of you would like to try it.'

'You can try it on me,' said Zuki, 'we've got to know if it works before we board one of those ships.'

'No, you won't,' Brond replied firmly, 'you are too valuable – I'll have a go.'

'You're sure?' asked Kono, Brond just nodded, 'let me know what you feel.'

Brond braced himself, not knowing quite what to expect – and then winced and double up, clutching his stomach.

'I've never been kicked by a mule, but I expect it would feel something like that,' he said, 'it was a gut-wrenching pain, and I felt weak all over – God knows what those other poor bastards felt with a full blast.'

'Well, that was just about a gentle as I can manage,' said Kono, 'just a little more should knock you out.'

'No, you bloody don't,' exclaimed Brond, taking a couple of steps back, and then realised distance made little difference.

'What do you think?' asked Zuki, 'shall we try and board one of the carriers? Do you think they may have hand weapons?'

'I think it's worth a try,' said Brond, still rubbing his abdomen, 'they must have realised by now that we could have blown them to bits if we had wished to – and we didn't, so that illustrates a little leniency on our part. At the first sign of aggression, give 'em a blast Kono.' Kono nodded, but the grin had gone.

Brond eased their ship close to one of the carriers and engaged the magnetic grapple. The satisfying clunk indicated that the alien carrier was largely made of steel or some metal which responded to magnetic fields, and now the two vessels were firmly locked together.

They were already suited up, so it was just a matter of adding their breather packs and helmets, and they were ready to go.

'I assume there will be an airlock of some kind on the carrier,' Brond commented as they entered their own air lock, 'otherwise we'll have to cut our way in.'

'I would assume so,' replied Zuki, 'I would expect only a couple of aliens to be on board - sort of maintenance crew, I somehow doubt they'll be armed.'

Using whatever hand holds they could find, the three of them worked their way along their ship and up onto the alien carrier.

'I would think their airlock would be on the underside of the carrier cradle,' Zuki said through the intercom, 'their crew would probably have their living quarters in the main section above the cradles – it wouldn't be efficient for them to travel large distances in the attack ships.'

They entered the huge cavity of one of the cradles, and worked their way up to the top, the light level dropping all the while.

'That looks like an airlock,' said Kono, 'it's got a lever to one side of it – give it a go?'

'Yep,' said Brond, 'but stay to one side of it, in case there's an atmosphere inside.'

Kono pulled the lever down, but nothing happened.

'Try pushing it up,' said Zuki, 'don't forget it's alien, and may not work as our things do.'

This time a pale blue light came on next to the lever, and then the man-sized hatchway opened a little. Kono gripped the edge of the hatch and swung it fully open.

'Looks like we're in.' said a somewhat surprised Kono, and stepped into the gloom of a short corridor, the others following behind him.

'Better shut that hatch, or the next one won't open.' said Zuki, switching on his torch.

The second hatch also had a lever, and then they were inside the alien carrier.

'I can hear our footsteps,' said Zuki, 'so that means we have an atmosphere, but I don't think we should breathe it – yet.'

The corridor branched in two, the left one leading to some steps up which they climbed, and reaching the top were confronted by another door.

'Well, we should be up in the top section of this thing by the number of steps we've taken,' said Brond, 'so watch out for aliens; the door's got a lever on it, so let's go in,' he added, pushing Kono forward.

The door opened, revealing a square room with metal walls, a long bench and what passed for a table attached to one wall. In front of them two humanoid figures stood next to each other, dressed in dull grey overalls with a bewildered look on their faces – but it was difficult to tell if they were really bewildered as they were alien, and somewhat ugly. Brond raised a hand to shoulder height, palm facing the pair, and waited for a response.

The two aliens looked at each other, and then raised their arms away from their bodies to indicate they were not armed or holding anything. He was taking no chances, and strode forward purposefully to pat them down for anything concealed, and having found nothing, stepped back to his companions.

'I don't suppose you speak our language?' he asked, hopefully.

A series of garbled grunts from one of the aliens confirmed the problems they were about to have.

'Better tie the ugly sods up,' Brond said, 'can't take a chance they might sabotage anything – or us.'

The aliens gave no resistance to being bound hand and foot, except for a few unintelligible grunts as Kono tightened one of the knots.

'Kono, you keep an eye on these two while Zuki and I take a look around and try to make some sense of this thing – any problems, just give 'em a little zap. Somehow we've got to get into conversation with 'em – but God knows how.'

After a while the pair returned from their exploration of the carrier's upper section with a bundle of rolled up charts, and Brond said the carrier didn't seem to be armed.

'As far as we can make out, these two are just maintenance personal, and possibly run the drive units – they are dressed differently to the ones we saw on the mining planet – I don't think they'll put up much of a fight. Our main problem will be trying to understand them – we've got to find out why they attacked us, and what they want.'

'Just had a thought,' said Zuki, 'Kono, can you pick up anything from these two, mentally I mean?'

'Not tried that,' Kono replied thoughtfully, 'could be worth a try, I suppose.'

Zuki and Brond looked on expectantly as Kono looked first at one alien, and then the other, both of which gave a little jerk as Kono's gaze flickered from one to the other.

'Couldn't get much,' said Kono, 'they seem very surprised to see us – can't figure how we got here, or something like that – they don't dislike us, but are afraid of what we might do. I think they are pretty low in the ranking stakes, or that's how they feel.'

'OK, here's what we'll do.' Said Brond, 'Sit 'em up on the bench by the table thing, I'll get what I think is their food from a little room we found – and see how they react to that.'

With the two aliens sitting forlornly on the bench, Brond put down what he thought was their food and a bottle of a pale grey fluid on the table.

'Right, undo their hands, and let's see what they do with that lot.'

Immediately the aliens ripped off what seemed to be a plastic covering from the food blocks Brond had put on the table, exposing a dull brown square of something which they devoured in great haste, and then took a good swig from the bottle of fluid.

Both looked up and opened their mouths slightly as they looked at their captors.

'Do you think they are asking for more, or are they saying 'thank you'?' asked Kono, 'and I wonder if they can eat our food – that's if we take them prisoner back to our planet – it might take a language expert to unravel the grunts they make – I can't make any sense of it.'

'If we can establish 'yes' and 'no', we might be able to use drawings to show them what we want,' offered Zuki, 'then perhaps we can get these carriers back in orbit around our planet. Our people might learn a lot from them, after all they have travelled a long way to get here – further than we can travel. I'll need a few food blocks and that liquid to do it.'

'That's good thinking,' Brond replied, 'OK, come up with a plan, and have a go – I'll get the necessaries.'

By offering and withdrawing the alien's food block with a nod or shake of the head reinforced with 'yes' and 'no', the aliens finally understood what was expected of them. Their verbal response was a little less eloquent, being more of a series of grunts than understandable language, and at the same time, they seemed to have lost their fear of the humans and seemed quite happy to co-operate.

Using sketch pads and copious nods and shaking of heads, it was finally got across to the aliens that the fleet of carriers were to be moved to an orbit around the human's main planet – but they never did find out how the aliens communicated with the other carriers to get the move underway. Base was informed of the event as the fleet began to move, and informed Brond that an alien attack ship had crash landed in a desert area on their home world, and wondered what to do about it. Brond suggested that they leave it where it was until he returned.

Slowly the alien carriers lined up and began the journey towards Zuki's home world, where they would be held in geostationary orbit until Brond's return. Meanwhile, Brond sent in a report indicating that the alien carrier fleet was on its way, and should be left alone when in orbit, until he and the others were able to board the vessels one by one, and collect the alien crews which would then be held in isolation until they could be interrogated.

'So far, things have worked out very well,' Zuki commented, 'but we really need to know what happened to the alien attack ships – we don't want them wandering about in our solar system.'

'Well, we know one of them crash-landed in one of our deserts, and I suppose the others would have just carried on in a straight line after Kono blasted them – I somehow doubt they are still alive, but we'd better make sure. I'll get Base on to it.'

By the time they had reached the orbiting space station and taken the shuttle down to planet side, the stress and strain they had been under began to show, and the leader of the Council after congratulating them on their efforts, ordered a three-day rest period.

Zuki's parents were overjoyed to see him again so soon, and did their best to make Kono feel welcome, despite their fear of what they thought he was capable of.

At long last, a report came in stating that the alien attack ships had passed through their system, and were heading out into deep space – still in a straight line, until they had disappeared from the long range detectors – except for one, which couldn't be accounted for.

The aliens from the carrier ships had been rounded up and were being held in the hidden mountain complex – awaiting a visit from Zuki and Co. One thing which did puzzle the guards was the fact that all the prisoners seemed quite docile and co-operative – somehow the first two must have communicated the fact that they had been treated quite well, but how this was done remained a mystery.

At last, the leave period came to an end, and Zuki and Kono were picked up by Brond with the promise of more leave when the next stage of the alien problem had been sorted out – but nothing specific was mentioned.

'And now the real fun can begin,' said Brond as they disembarked from the transport at the complex, 'we have acquired a couple of language experts, but I think it'll need a little help from you, Zuki – you seem to have made some progress with 'em up on their ship. Are you willing to continue?'

'Yes, sure,' Zuki replied, not knowing just how he would set about it.

The trio entered the interrogation room to find the aliens seated at a long table, and looking quite happy with their lot – although it was difficult to judge exactly what they were feeling.

'We've had their food and drink analysed,' Brond offered, 'and managed to produce something which is essentially the same, although it looks a little different. Hope it doesn't kill 'em before we find out just what they intended to do; so, let's get on with it.'

'All we've established so far,' said Zuki, 'is 'yes' and 'no'. I think, using sketch pads, we should be able to find out a little more, but it's going to be difficult.'

'If you need to put a little pressure on, I can give 'em a zap.' Kono said, wanting to contribute something to the event.

'Let's see what we can do with gentle persuasion first, then you can have a go.' Brond said, hoping it wouldn't come to that.

Zuki made a sketch of one of the carriers, and then two pictures of the attack ships which he cut out, and put to one side. The carrier picture was pushed across the table in front of the aliens, and they all craned forward to look at it. Zuki then pushed the attack ship pictures into position on the carrier picture, and waited for some response.

All the aliens nodded in unison, almost like synchronized dolls – and that was a bit unnerving to the five humans who were looking on.

'God, they're like bloody robots.' Kono muttered under his breath.

Zuki said, 'yes' loudly, and the alien nearest the picture replied 'zzes.'

Zuki then moved one of the attack pictures out from the carrier and along the table some way. 'Yes' he said.

'Nozz' the alien replied, and put the attack ship picture back on the carrier, and then moved both attack pictures out across the table together.

'Right – got that,' said Brond, 'they move out as synchronized pairs, but how can we find out their intentions after that?'

Zuki then made a picture of their world, and placed the two attack ships up against it.

The aliens looked at one another, and the one in the middle who had spoken before, raised his shoulders and dropped them again.

'Looks like they don't know what the ships are supposed to do,' said Brond, 'surely they must have some idea?'

'Let's give them a little reward for their efforts,' said Zuki, 'a small portion of their food and a drink.'

A piece of food and a small beaker of drink were placed before each alien, who greedily consumed them, and then looked up expectantly.

Zuki made a sketch of a carrier alien and placed it on one of the attack pictures.

'Nozz' said the alien, shaking his head, and picked up the picture and placed it on the carrier. 'Yezz' he added.

'Although they look similar to those in the attack ships and not so ugly, they are dressed differently,' Brond said, 'and aren't aggressive – I wouldn't mind betting they are a sub species, perhaps assigned to more menial tasks, like manning the carriers.'

'Certainly looks that way,' said Zuki, 'they don't seem to want to be associated with the attack ships.'

The two language experts looked glum, as they couldn't find anything to add to the proceedings.

'How about doing some pictures of the attack ships attacking our world – complete with explosions,' said Kono, 'and see how they react to that.'

Zuki did as suggested, but the aliens only reaction was to look at each other and the spokesman just said 'Nozz'.

'They are either acting dumb,' said one of the language experts, 'or really don't know what the others intended.'

'Want me to give 'em a zap?' asked Kono, enthusiastically.

'Not just yet,' Brond replied calmly, 'but it might come to that.'

'I don't think we're going to get much more from this lot,' said Zuki, 'how about we visit the site where the alien ship crashed? That might give us a little more to go on.'

The aliens were ushered out to their quarters, and the trio left for the transport which would take them to the desert area where the alien ship had crashed earlier.

The pilot put in the co-ordinates for the crashed alien ship, and they were on their way. The desert area took up almost a half of the planet's land mass, rolling mounds of sand interspersed with craggy outcrops of dark rock, like black fingers pointing up to the sky. As the site of the crash came into view, they could see a ring of military personal had surrounded the ship, but at a respectful distance.

'That's not a posting I would have chosen,' said Brond, as their cruiser prepared to land, 'apart from the heat, they must be bored out of their minds with just sand and an inert lump of metal to look at.'

'Now that's interesting,' said Zuki, craning his neck to get a better view of the alien ship, 'it seems almost intact, although a little battered. That thing isn't intended for a planetary landing – they used a shuttle to reach the mining planet.'

Their cruiser swung around for the final landing approach, and that was when the mystery was solved.

'They must have used reverse thrust to slow the ship down after it was caught by the planet's mass,' Zuki commented, 'and somehow they kept it from falling like a stone. That was one dammed good pilot they must have had, he managed to bring it in to hit the top of that massive sand dune and it slid all the way down to the bottom, losing its momentum as it did so. If I hadn't seen it, I wouldn't have believed it possible.'

As they debarked, a high-ranking military officer greeted them with a very smart salute.

'We have been instructed to destroy that thing if there is any aggressive move, or if anything tries to leave it,' he said, 'although I don't see how there can be any survivors by the state of it.'

'I would agree with that,' Brond replied, 'but you never know - that thing must be made of something a lot tougher than anything we have. The research boys will have a field day taking it apart, I would think.'

The four of them walked around the alien ship, looking for a means of entry, but as the outer hull was so distorted and burnt, they found none.

'Looks like we'll have to cut our way in,' Zuki offered, 'how about we clamp a microphone to the hull and see if we can pick up any sounds? If there are any survivors, they won't come out peacefully.'

'The tech boys will have something, I'm sure,' the officer replied, 'I'll get them on to it right away.'

A microphone plus amplifier appeared as if by magic and was applied to the battered hull, but the only sounds they could pick up were made by their own movements, so it was deemed that those aboard were all dead.

'Do you think flame cutting equipment will get us in,' asked Zuki, 'bearing in mind the cooking that thing got when it entered our atmosphere? I think we'll need diamond cutters to gain entry.'

'I'll get some flown in right away,' said the officer, and hurried away to do so.

Brond picked up one of the very few stones among the mountains of sand which surrounded them, and gave the alien hull a hearty thump.

'Now that's odd,' he commented, 'I would have expected that to have produced some sort of metal ring, being metal. It's as though I had just hit a lump of dough – no sound at all – so what the hell is that thing made of?'

The following day, the cutting tools arrived. Zuki was eager to get inside the alien ship, helping to carry the equipment over to the battered hulk, and the secrets it might contain.

With the cutter on its mounting frame up against the hull, the power button was pressed by Brond, and the motor roared into life. As the cutting blade touched the hull, the motor whined as it came under full load, but the blade seemed to slow down, the shimmering diamond teeth glittering in the sunlight.

'Withdraw the cutter!' Brond yelled, 'Something's not right, it's hardly made a mark.'

Sure enough, the cutter had barely scratched the surface of the alien craft, a shallow groove being the only evidence of their attempt to enter the alien ship, the edges of which looked as if the had been melted.

'What the hell is that stuff,' was all Brond could say, frustrated, 'it looks as if the material has melted and tried to stick to the cutting blade.'

The power was cut, and the motor slowed down, and then stopped. Zuki went up close to the hull and examined the shallow groove, giving the edge a tap with a metal bar.

'I know this sounds silly, but let's try again, but this time dribble some water where the blade meets the hull. It looks as if the material melts and then crystallises - the water should make it crystallise before it forms a gooey mess and it should then clear the cut.'

A drum of water was brought up to the hull, a small pump attached, and the nozzle clamped into position such that the flow would meet the blade as it bit into the hull.

The blade spun up to full speed, a shimmering disc in the bright sunlight, and an ear-piercing screech signalled some degree of success, as a mist of fine particles flew off the hull.

'Stand well back,' Brond yelled, 'we don't know what that stuff is, and it might be poisonous – so don't breathe it in.'

The spinning blade continued to breach the alien hull, the machine giving a little lurch as it finally broke through, accompanied by a sharp hiss as the internal atmosphere of the ship bled out. The machine operator then put his hand on the lever to lower the blade to make a vertical cut, looking up at Brond for a signal to do so. Brond nodded his head, and the screeching began again.

By midday they had cut a square section out of the hull, quickly pulling the cutter out of the way as the section of hull fell to the sand below.

'We don't now what atmosphere they used,' said Brond, 'so we'd better use breathing masks until we know what we have in there.'

Zuki, Brond, and an apprehensive Kono were about to enter the alien ship, when the officer in command of the operation suggested that one of his men should lead the team, fully armed.

'I very much doubt there is anything alive in that heap,' Brond retorted, 'that which wasn't cooked upon re-entry would have been flattened by the impact of landing – I think we are best suited to deal with this sort of thing, we've met this lot before.'

The commander looked disappointed, but acquiesced reluctantly.

Someone had thoughtfully produced a six-step mounting block, and Brond gingerly stepped up into the opening in the alien craft.

'Seems OK,' he called out, 'watch out for loose items on the floor, all sorts of things have been shaken loose.'

Their hand lamps lit up a dull metallic scene – nothing had been painted, at least not in colour, and it gave a grim, austere look to the ship. The trio were in a square shaped room, with what looked like a door or hatchway into the rest of the ship.

'This looks like an air lock of some kind,' commented Brond, looking around, 'and that is the way into the main ship,' pointing to a panel set in the main bulkhead, 'those two knobs are probably the means of controlling it – but without power we may have a problem.'

Zuki moved up to the panel for a closer look, and hopefully pressed both knobs, but nothing happened.

'There's a small gap on this side,' he said, 'and it looks as if the locking cleats have been sprung loose, we might be able to prise it open with a metal bar.'

A bar was passed up to them, and Zuki put all his weight behind it, but the panel would not open.

'Here, let's all get on the end of it,' said Brond, 'otherwise we'll have to get that cutting machine in here, and that could be difficult.'

With the three of them heaving together, there was a couple of sharp cracks as the last cleats gave way, and the panel swung open.

The three lamps lit up a scene of ultimate carnage – pieces of bodies lay all over the floor, most of which reminded them of those found after one of Kono's mind blasts on the old mining planet. But three seemed to have evaded the mind blast, and were intact, apart from being somewhat twisted and very dead.

'That's odd,' stated Brond, 'those three haven't ripped themselves apart, so how did they survive Kono's blast?'

'This must be the ship that almost got away,' said Zuki, 'and Kono had to give it another shot. Maybe these three were in a part of the ship shielded from the mind blast and were able to control it to some extent. The gravity of our home world captured it, and they did their best to land here.'

The horrific scene must have got to Kono, who tried to suppress his feelings, but not before they all felt a surge of nausea – as did those outside the ship.

'Better get a team in here and clear up this mess,' said Brond, 'pass the word back – I don't envy them the job though.'

Moving the lamps around, they could see benches along the walls, and racks of assorted weapons above them.

'This is where they must have sat,' said Kono, 'waiting to land and attack – ugly looking sods if that one is anything to go by,' pointing to a severed head, 'the old saying 'really look at a person and it will tell you what they're like' seems to be true for this lot.'

They squelched their way through the remains of the dismembered aliens, and reached another hatchway which had a handle attached.

'Why does that one have a sensible handle and the outer one had buttons?' asked a somewhat puzzled Kono.

'I expect the buttoned door had an interlock such that it couldn't be opened accidentally,' Brond replied, 'if it was opened when the outer hatch was open it would bleed all the air out of the ship – I would have thought you would have worked that out.' And then regretted what he had said – no way was he going to intentionally upset Kono.

The next section they entered seemed to be a passage with storerooms on either side. Zuki couldn't help his curiosity getting the better of him, and opened a door. As far as they could tell, it was a food store – containing the same sort of packages they had found on the carrier ship.

'By the quantity here, I think they were in for a very long haul,' said Brond, 'I would suggest you be careful which doors you open. God knows what might be behind 'em.'

After leaving the stores, they found themselves in what Brond considered to be the power plant which drove the ship. Two massive humps on the floor, each side of the walkway, looked suitably menacing – a series of large conduits radiating out from them finally disappear into floor after passing through a couple of cylindrical lumps, which felt warm when Brond touched them.

'Our boys will have field day going through this lot – I don't know if it was the carriers or these ships which could travel through interstellar space, but that is a drive unit we would very much like to have.'

At the far end of the engine room they were faced with a blank wall – just solid metal, and no sign of a hatch or door.

'This looks like a spiral stairway in that corner,' said Zuki, 'shall we go up?'

'Why not, that's what we're here for. But be careful,' Brond replied.

Zuki led the way up the spiral, only to stop at the top.

'Got another door here,' he called out, 'but there's no handle or buttons.'

Brond pushed past him, running his fingers all over the surface, feeling for lumps or bumps which might activate it – but there was nothing.

'It's got to have some means of opening,' said a frustrated Brond, 'all doors do.'

'Maybe it slides to one side,' said Kono, 'but how do you grip it to do so?'

'Got an idea,' said Zuki, 'I'll put my lamp on the floor so that the light shines upwards, that'll show up any differences in the door's surface.' And did so.

'Well, I'll be damned,' exclaimed Brond, 'it looks like a greasy patch where a hand has been placed many times – why didn't it show up when I shone my lamp on it?'

'Something to do with the angle of the light and the surface of the door, I would suspect,' Zuki replied, 'but I'm not sure just what. I'll give it a try.'

He placed is hand firmly on the patch and moved it to one side, and the door slid open.

Brond muttered several expletives which were only just audible.

'If that is a sensor plate, and the power's off, how the hell does it work?' asked Kono, 'it doesn't make sense to me.'

'That's something the research boys will have to find out,' Zuki said, 'but it seems to work.'

They shone their lights around the small room now exposed, and all three gasped as one.

Chapter 6
The Alien

SEATED IN AN odd-looking chair was a hunched-up alien, seemingly in one piece, and surrounded by controls and several viewing screens.

'So that's the pilot,' exclaimed Brond, 'I wonder why he's stuck in here instead of having a clear viewing port like we do?'

'Well, they are aliens, and probably do things differently to us.' Zuki replied.

It was a bit crowded, but all three managed to squeeze into the tiny control room.

'Looks like he banged his head on the controls when the ship crashed,' Zuki offered, 'otherwise he's intact. Looks like a bump on his forehead and a smear of what they use for blood. It looks brown, but maybe that's the light.'

What surprised the other two was Kono, who bent forward and moved the alien's head back into its normal position.

'Surely the body would be stiff – rigour mortis should have set in long ago.' Brond said.

'Maybe it's not dead,' said Zuki, 'just unconscious or in a coma. It's not cold,' he added, placing his hand on the creature's head, 'God, that feels odd – it's sort of rough, or gritty.'

'Right, I'm going to get some cord to tie it up,' Brond said, 'God knows what it might do if it comes around.' And with that, he disappeared down the spiral stairway with indecent haste.

With the alien trussed up like a Christmas turkey, two of the security staff were detailed to carefully remove it from its chair, and out of the ship.

'There's not a lot more we can do here, this hulk is for the research boys to take apart bit by bit. We should learn a lot from this,' said Brond, 'so let's return to base with our alien. The medics might be able to bring it back to life, and then we'll have a chance to interrogate the little sod.'

The journey back to base was uneventful, except Kono was shaking slightly, and not looking very happy.

When they arrived, the alien was rushed off to the medical centre with Zuki in attendance to explain what had happened to it, and what he thought was the best way of reviving it, but no one was too keen to get near it.

The trio met up in the canteen to discuss what to do next, and Brond thought it might be useful to see what the linguists had achieved with the twelve aliens from the carriers.

'Well, we have done quite well,' one of them said, 'we have 'yes' and 'no', 'new' and 'old' by showing them a manky bit of their food and a fresh piece. Using pictures, we have established that they are quite peaceful, but do not really like the others who attacked us. They seem to be of the same race, but a different caste. We have decoded many other words, and have recorded their sounds so that you can play them back to them for questioning. We hear that you have one of the attacking aliens, so you should be able to question it using our recordings.'

Brond thanked then for their efforts, and the three of them then went to the medical centre to see what progress had been made.

The chief medical officer greeted them with a worried look on his face.

'We have detected a heartbeat, but it is very slow and weak – well, compared to ours. A mixture of their food and drink has been feed to it via a tube, but there is very little else we can do. The lump on its head has gone down a little since it arrived, but it still seems to be in a deep coma.'

'Let us know as soon as it shows any sign of life,' said Brond, 'it's the only alien from the attacking force we have, and we want to know why they attacked us, and if any more are likely to turn up.'

'I've had an idea,' said Zuki, Brond and Kono looked apprehensively at each other, wondering what was coming next.

'When I had that light experience back in the cave, I found I had enhanced abilities afterwards – I wonder if you have some ability to do with reaching into another's mind, Kono.'

'Don't know, haven't thought about it,' Kono replied, 'I am able to manage my thoughts a little better. What did you have in mind?'

'See if you can reach into our minds – get a picture of what we're thinking of – if you can, that would be very useful when we interrogate the alien – if it survives.'

'Don't know if I can do that, but I'll give it a try – you sure you want to do this?'

'Yes.' Zuki replied, but Brond didn't look too sure.

'OK, you two think of something. Hold the picture steady, and I'll try to pick it up.'

All was silent for a while, and then Kono hesitatingly said,

'It's a bit hazy, but Zuki is looking at his old village – a little row of thatched houses – that's all; I can't get anything from you, Brond.'

'Not surprised,' Brond replied, 'I was just looking at a blackness, I'll try something else.'

'I get a faint picture of our alien,' Kono said after a few moments, 'but it's not very clear, and it keeps changing. I'm not too sure I want to dip into the aliens' mind though. Anyway Zuki, can you see other people's pictures?' he added.

'No, I can't, but I can pick up how they are feeling, to some extent.' Zuki replied.

As Zuki had accomplished all that had been asked of him, he enquired if he could have some more leave to see his parents. Brond's response was 'not just yet – the alien might regain consciousness, and we'll need you to be on hand for interrogation.'

Zuki and Kono spent the next three days exploring the complex, puzzled that some areas were 'out of bounds' for no apparent reason, but getting a general idea of what the complex was all about.

Brond joined them to announce the news that the research team had tried analysing the outer hull of the alien ship, and although they didn't recognise the material, concluded it was of some form of protection from the hard radiation of space and high speed particles. Another team were having a hard time of it trying to dismantle the ship's drive to see how it worked, and were getting nowhere fast. One thing that did puzzle the researchers was the fact that the dismembered bodies of the aliens should have shown signs of decomposition by now, and they hadn't.

The trio were about to go to the canteen yet again, when one of the medics came rushing up to say that the alien looked as if it might come to at any moment. As they entered the room where the alien was being kept, a deep grunt was heard, and the alien's head twitched.

Brond was about to ask if the alien was held securely, when he noticed the metal clamps holding its arms and legs firmly to the surgical table.

'Has it done anything else apart from that grunt?' he asked.

'No sir,' came the reply from one of the medics, 'it did move its head a few times, so we thought we'd better call you. The heart rate has gone up, and it's breathing more deeply now.'

'Make sure you keep it securely held,' Brond added, 'it's quite heavily built and probably very strong. God knows what it would do if it got loose. We'll be back tomorrow to see how it's doing – if anything else happens, let us know at once – day or night.'

With nothing else to do, Zuki and Kono went to see the aliens who had come from the carrier ships. Upon entering the room, they all got up from the benches they were sitting on, and held their arms out to their sides. Zuki motioned them to be seated again, and after a bit of confusion, one of them cottoned on as to what was expected of them and sat down, the others following immediately.

Zuki asked for an audio amplifier, the speech discs and the translation sheets, so that he could question the aliens, and these were quickly produced by one of the attendants.

By looking at the translation sheet, he could see their words and the number assigned to the grunt like noise the aliens emitted, and was thus able to enter the numbers into the machine to make a crude question or sentence.

First Zuki asked where they came from, and the largest alien, who seemed to be their spokesman, pointed towards the ceiling and uttered a grunt. The machine did its best to translate and came up with 'big distance.' A star map was quickly produced by the attendant. Upon showing it to the alien, it shook its head, indicating that they came from somewhere well off the map, but was unable to elaborate further.

He then asked why they had come – and through the translator he got 'they didn't know – they just went where they were told to go.'

'I don't think we're going to get anything meaningful from this lot,' Zuki said to Kono, who just nodded his head, 'perhaps a little pressure on the one we got from the crashed ship might get us somewhere.' At which point Kono brightened up considerably.

At this point, Brond entered the room and enquired what they were doing. He didn't like being left out of such things, and showed it. After explaining that they were unable to get much information from the carrier aliens, Zuki suggested they try the one from the crashed ship.

'That's what I've come about,' said Brond, 'the medics say the alien has recovered somewhat – insofar that it is grunting loudly and trying to beak free from its restraints. This could be a good time to try and get some answers from it, even if we have to use force.'

'I think a little subtlety might be needed,' Zuki replied, 'if we can show it that we mean no harm, it may be more co-operative. We can use Kono if all else fails.'

'Alright,' said Brond, 'you know more about these creatures than I do, but I'd like to squeeze the little sod 'till its eyeballs fly out. Don't forget what it did to our miners, and they offered no resistance.'

The three of them entered the room containing the complaining alien, who stopped grunting and struggling as soon as they came in, and gave them a glare which would have struck fear in lesser men. The alien creature had been stripped of its clothing, and looked even more unpleasant than before, its shin having broken in several places and oozing a dark brown liquid.

Zuki ordered the alien's food and drink to be brought in, and then cut off a small portion off the food block and poured out a small portion of the drink.

The translation equipment was set up, and Zuki got to work.

First, he established 'yes' and 'no' as he had done before. Then, glancing down the translation sheet, he keyed in the numbers to represent the phrase 'you want food/drink', hit the 'go' button, and sat back to see what would happen.

An unintelligible series of grunts followed, none of which the machine could translate, and he got another hateful glare for his trouble.

'Right,' said Zuki firmly, 'make sure he can't get out of his restraints. Be certain the vision monitors are manned at all times, and everyone leaves the room. Then put the lights out until you hear from us again.'

'What's the point of that?' Brond enquired quietly, 'get Kono to give it a couple of whacks, that should loosen its tongue.'

'You might think so, but I doubt it. It's losing moisture from where the skin has broken and the feed tube has been withdrawn, so it won't be long before its body will be screaming out for sustenance. That's when we offer it a little food and drink, but only a little. It will soon learn that co-operation will be rewarded – and unintelligible grunts will only mean another day without light, food or drink.'

'Hmm, I'm glad you're on our side,' Brond conceded, 'Let's hope it works.'

Just then an engineer from the team who were dismantling the alien ship came up to Brond, quietly spoke to him, and then left.

'Seems like we have a sort of break through,' Brond said, 'the engineers have dismantled the vision units from the alien ship and found them to be modular in construction. This means it's a plug-in system, which makes it easier for us to see how each piece works. Want to have a look at it?'

'You bet,' replied Zuki, 'it'll be interesting to see how different their systems are from ours – bearing in mind the flow of electrons is the same throughout the universe.'

'What do you mean? asked Brond, a puzzled look on his face.

'Wherever you are, electrons follow the same rules,' Zuki said, 'it's how we use them that will be different – should be interesting.'

Minutes later they were in a large room with a series of benches in the middle, and on these were the dismantled units from the alien ship. Fortunately, a bright engineer had the foresight to mark the linking cables up such that they would be able to connect them up correctly to the different modules, and Zuki sought out the man responsible to give him a 'well done' for his thoughtfulness.

'We have one main problem,' said one of the engineers, 'we don't know what voltage to apply to the system, as the ship's power system was not working and we were unable to sample the supply voltage or current to the setup.'

Zuki went to each module in turn, closely examining them as the covers had been removed.

'Their components look different to ours, and I don't recognise any of them,' he stated, 'have you looked for any replacement components? They should have some tucked away somewhere in case they have to do a repair. If you find any, we can test them to see what they do, and that will enable us to see if any of it makes sense.'

Two men were immediately dispatched to begin the search for spare components, while Zuki and the others went from unit to unit, trying to fathom how it all worked.

The following day, the trio returned to the interrogation room to see how the alien was faring. They decided he was not looking very happy.

The translation equipment was switched on, and Zuki tried again to get a reasonable response from their captive. The machine grunted the same message as before, and this time the alien nodded its head, and the machine emitted a 'yes'.

Zuki cut a small piece from the alien's food block, and poured out a little liquid from the container, passing it over to the alien. Although it was bound securely to its chair, they had left its arms free, and it eagerly grabbed the drink and swallowed it in one gulp. The slither of food followed, and the alien held out its hands for more.

'We'll try another question.' said Zuki, 'That went quite well, I think it's got the idea.'

Zuki punched in the numbers for 'where are you from?' The machine paused for a moment, and then issued a series of grunts. The alien just glared at them, and placed its arms on the table.

'OK,' said Zuki patiently, 'lights out and everybody leave, we'll meet again tomorrow – same time.'

And with that they left the alien to his own thoughts, in total darkness.

The following morning, they went to the engineers to see it they had found any components from the alien ship – and they had. Several containers, each holding an assortment of each component type.

'Right,' said Zuki, 'I'll need a twelve-volt DC power supply, and the usual array of test instruments that you would use yourselves.'

Half an hour later and Zuki had labelled each type of component, except for two, and these would remain a mystery for some time to come.

'You should be able to work out the circuit by comparing the labelled items against those in the actual unit – unless you find some of the ones I can't identify. It will at least give you some idea of what does what. Try powering up one of the units starting at five volts, and then gradually increase it to it twelve. Don't go above twelve volts. One of the alien components blew at fifteen volts, but twelve should be OK.'

Brond asked the engineers if they had tried to access the main power plant of the ship, and were told that they couldn't even get the main covers of it – but would advise him should they do so.

'Right,' said Zuki, 'it's time we paid our alien friend another visit. It should be quite thirsty by now, and perhaps a little more willing to co-operate.'

'Wouldn't put money on it,' Brond replied, grumpily, 'I'm all for putting a bit of pressure on it.' And he made a gesture of putting his hands around an imaginary throat.

The table at which the alien had been seated was firmly anchored to the floor, and its arms clamped to the tabletop. It couldn't even scratch an itching part of its body, and there must have been plenty of those with the skin lesions.

'My God,' exclaimed Brond, 'that's one awful stink,' he said, as they entered the room of the alien's incarceration.

'Probably its leaking body fluids are breaking down,' Zuki suggested, 'someone put the fans on.'

The alien was slumped forward, its head resting on the table, and as they approached it the head rose up, but the hateful glare was missing.

Zuki began with the food and drink question, and got a slow nod and a grunt, and a 'yes' from the translator. This time he gave the alien a slightly larger piece of its food and a half full mug of it drink, while one of the assistants freed the alien's arms from the holding clamps.

Zuki put in the code for 'will you answer questions', and sat back, arms folded across his chest, implying he had all the time in the world.

The alien looked up at Zuki and then the empty mug, and back to Zuki, who just nodded his head. The alien paused for a moment, and then nodded.

The star map had been extended somewhat, and was now put before the alien, and the machine asked, 'where are you from?'

Again, a long pause, as if the alien was weighing up the benefits of giving up some information in exchange for some much-needed nourishment. A long horny finger pointed to a star system, right on the edge of the map.

'Hell fire,' exclaimed Brond, 'that's one hell of a way away. So why did they pick on us, and how did they find us in the first place?'

'Maybe they have very sensitive detection equipment,' Zuki replied, 'and picked up our radio waves – which would indicate a civilised planet. Surely there must be other suitable worlds nearer their home planet – I would have thought. I'll see if I can find out.'

'Why did you pick on us?' proved difficult, as there not the suitable words available on the word exchange chart.

'Why this world?' was put into the translator, and the alien issued a series of grunts which was too much for the translator, which finally said 'you – me – you – me,' a long pause, and then 'want.'

'What the hell does that mean?' said Brond, 'Does it mean it wants us?'

'I think it means it wants what we have – our world – or something we have, maybe,' replied Zuki, 'Get some of the mineral we were getting from the mining planet. It might be that.'

The alien was given some more food and drink as a reward for its reply, which was gulped down greedily. Some while later a few pieces of the shiny mineral were brought in and put before the alien, which then nodded its head, and the machine said 'yes.'

'So, the silly sods were quite happy to destroy us all just for some minerals,' Brond almost shouted, 'well they bit off a bit more than they can chew.'

'I wonder why it was so important to them?' Zuki asked, 'It's only some rare earth metals. What we need to do is find out what they used it for, and that may not be so easy. But I'll try.'

'Why you want this?' was put into the translator, and a series of grunts came out.

The alien looked up at Zuki, but said nothing – just shook its head. The question was put again, and got the same result.

'Either it doesn't know, or won't say,' Kono said, with a knowing grin, 'I might be able to make it change its mind.'

'We'll give it one more chance,' Zuki replied, 'and then you can have a go – OK?'

The question was put again, but there was no response, so Zuki ordered 'everyone out along with the lights, we'll see what two days will do.' And with that they left the alien to reconsider its response.

'I know we use that ore ourselves,' said Brond, as they left the interrogation room, 'but there's nothing spectacular in it, as far as I know.'

'Maybe it's what they do with it,' Zuki replied, 'and that's what I intend to find out, one way or another.'

The trio marched along the seemingly endless corridors until they reached the canteen, and stopped for welcome refreshments.

'I don't know how that thing can go so long without food and water,' Brond said, 'I know I couldn't – I'd be only too willing to tell anyone anything in its position.'

'I did pick up one feeling just now,' said Kono, 'that it's terrified of telling us something it knows – you could work on that, Zuki. Apart from that, its thoughts are cold – no emotion that I could pick up – no feeling for itself, or anyone else. Hence the brutal killing of our miners, they were no threat to anyone.'

'I am slowly coming around to your way of thinking, Kono.' said Zuki, 'Blast the little sod. But the data we could obtain is far more important than my feelings.'

Brond just nodded his head – he understood.

Just as Zuki was about say something, one of the engineers working on the alien craft burst into the canteen.

'Thought you ought to know, we've got the cover off one of those big humps in the ship – we think you ought to come and have a look.'

'Why us?' asked Brond, 'you guys are the engineers.'

'Sorry Sir, with no disrespect, we really mean Zuki, sir.'

'It's just Zuki,' Zuki said, 'no need for the sir – it's my given name.'

'Sorry Zuki, would you come please?'

'Yes, of course,' Zuki replied, 'shall we go gentlemen?'

The trio got up and joined the engineer, who almost ran out to the transport.

Half an hour later, and they were at the crash site, and scrambled into the alien craft.

Chapter 7
A New Power

'Right,' said Brond, 'so what's the problem?'

'That thing,' said one of the engineers, pointing to a large half submerged metallic hoop, 'we've sent for a fusion specialist – he should be here any moment. Although we have never managed to make a fusion generator, it looks like it might be one.'

Zuki and Kono's eyes opened wide, and Brond muttered a little used expletive.

'If that's what it is,' said an astonished Brond, 'and we can get it to work and then duplicate it, that's just about the biggest gift we could get.'

Just then the specialist arrived, and was introduced around. He took one look at the huge loop of the torus, and shook his head.

'We have a torus, but it's enormous – you can't make one this small – it just wouldn't work.'

'Well, someone has,' said Kono, with a grin, 'otherwise this ship wouldn't have got here.'

'I must admit, it's producing something by the size of those power cables,' said the expert, 'but I don't see how it can be a fusion generator. Where are the magnetic coils and all the other bits and pieces you would need?'

'Perhaps the aliens have found another way to do it,' said Zuki, 'just because we haven't done it yet doesn't mean it can't be done. As you say, it's producing an awful lot of something, and I suspect that's what the drive units use. They wouldn't need this just to power up the lights and electrics. I think we need to expose the ships drive and see if these cables lead to it.'

The expert shuffled to the back of the group, and when no one was looking, made his exit – somewhat crestfallen, and well out of his depth.

'I think we should get the engineers to strip away some of this flooring so that we can trace those cables.' said Zuki, 'I wonder if they shut off the power just before they crashed, or maybe there is an inertia switch which cuts the power on impact – otherwise the whole thing might blow up.'

There was nothing else they could contribute until the engineers had done their bit, so they returned to the research complex to try and figure out a way to make the alien a little more compliant.

'Two days is quite a long time to leave it without fluids,' said Zuki, 'so someone must keep watch on it all the time, using infrared. We don't want it to die on us, not until we have obtained all the information we can get.'

'Do you think they will send others if this lot don't return?' asked Brond, 'We've got away with it this time, but I wouldn't like to go through it again. Anyway, how the hell did they find us in the first place?'

'We may find out, if we can get the little sod to talk,' Zuki replied, 'and I mean to do just that.'

'Well, they're humanoid, like us,' said Brond, 'apart from being a damned sight uglier. So, what works for us should work on them,'

'Not necessarily,' Zuki replied, 'it's a mental thing, I suspect. They may have bodies like us, but they are a little more advanced scientifically, and I'll bet they don't have our way of looking at things – if the mining planet is anything to go by.'

'There's not much else we can do with the alien until the day after tomorrow, that's if it's still alive then. So, lets see how the boys with the alien vision system are getting on.'

As they entered the research room, they were greeted with a bunch of happy faces.

'We've figured out how this thing works,' said one of the engineers, 'and built our own version – and it works! Not only that, it's better than our system. We are now trying to work out how the controls down to the drive units work, and if we can do that, and we can duplicate the power plant and drive units – we will have deep space travel. Just like they have.'

'That makes me even more determined to squeeze that alien.' said Zuki, 'We may well need that ability, if they come back again.'

'I think we all need some time to relax.' said Brond, 'But we can't leave the complex in case the alien throws a wobbly, and we'll need you here for that, Zuki. Sorry.'

Zuki and Kono took the lift to the outside world, such as it was. The complex was built underneath the bottom of what looked like an extinct volcano with mountains all around, so when they reached the surface all they could see were rock walls in all directions, and the sky above.

'They certainly chose this place well.' said Kono, 'Even if you fell into the crater, you'd never know what lay beneath it, and by the looks of it, this place has been in operation for some considerable time. I wonder what else they do here?'

'I doubt they'll tell us, even if we ask,' Zuki replied wistfully, 'but I'd really like to know. How about we have a little poke about?' Kono agreed, enthusiastically.

Zuki must have pressed the wrong button, for the lift carried on two levels below where they had started from.

The lift stopped with a judder, and the pair got out into a dimly lit corridor which stretched off in both directions. All along the walls, grilled doors were set back half a metre or so into the bedrock. They peered into some of them, but as there were no internal lights, little detail was visible.

'These look like prison cells,' Zuki said, 'but they don't look as if they have been used. I wonder who they were intended for.'

'Could be for any aliens we captured,' replied Kono, 'bearing in mind we have been attacked before. But that was some time ago.'

'You were involved in that?' Zuki said, 'What actually happened?'

'We managed to capture a couple of aliens alive, and several of us were ordered to interrogate them – using any means we could think of – just get results. We weren't getting anywhere using ordinary methods, so we applied a bit of pressure – well, quite a lot really. One of the aliens died, and the other one had some sort of fit, and blew his mind. I don't remember much about it, except it killed two of my fellow operatives and left me with an affliction which can't be cured. So, I was dumped on that world you found me on; I was supplied with food and anything else I needed – except company – and I missed that. You have no idea how pleased I was after a while, when you didn't seem to be affected.'

Even in the dim light of the corridor, Zuki could see Kono's eyes were wet, and gave him a hug.

'We've managed to correct it somewhat,' said Zuki, 'and I'm sure we will be able to sort it out fully, in time. Let's go back to the upper levels. I find it very depressing down here, and there's nothing else to see.'

They both went to see how the alien was getting on, and could see on the viewing screen its head was resting on the tabletop between its manacled hands. A slow rising and falling of its chest indicated that it was still alive, and Zuki hoped he had judged his two-day timing right.

Brond joined them for the evening meal, and Zuki asked him about the prison cells, but Brond changed the subject after saying he knew little about them. Zuki then said he would continue his interrogation of the alien first thing in the morning, as it looked a bit weak earlier, and he didn't want to push his luck too far. Brond agreed.

Straight after breakfast, the trio descended to the interrogation room, and for a heart stopping moment Zuki thought he had got it wrong, as the alien didn't move as they approached. Kono banged his fist hard on the table, and the alien slowly looked up.

Zuki tapped in the code for 'will you talk to us?', the machine emitted several unintelligible grunts, and the alien nodded slowly. A small portion of food and drink was then put before the wretched creature, who consumed it eagerly.

Tapping in 'why you want the minerals?' got no response for a few moments, and then the alien grunted back. The translator did its best with 'for ship'. More food and drink.

'What part of ship?' was tapped in – again a wait, and then the machine said 'the energy maker.'

'What part of the energy maker?' brought back 'the ring.'

'God, this is like pulling teeth,' said Zuki.

'Which mineral?' uttered the translator in a series of grunts.

The alien raised both hands a short distance up from the table, the manacles rattling as it did so, and slowly shook its head from side to side.

'It doesn't know,' muttered Kono, 'I picked that up.'

'Why you kill us?' was asked. The alien just looked at Zuki, and didn't say anything.

A full beaker of drink was pushed forward, just outside the alien's reach, and the question asked again.

This got 'you stop us' from the translator.

'You ask – we give you' brought a surprised expression on the alien's face, or so they thought.

The alien lowered its gaze, blankly looking at the tabletop, its head very slowly going from side to side.

'I think it's realised its mistake,' said Brond, 'the killing was unnecessary. Give the silly sod its drink,' and Zuki did so.

The questioning went on all morning, until all were tired, but many questions were answered to the team's satisfaction.

'OK,' said Zuki, 'the language experts should have got the hang of it by now, they can carry on building up the translations. There's still a lot more we need to know.'

'We've still got a lot of its food and drink left,' said Brond, 'and I'll get it analysed. It won't last forever.' And with that, he got up and left.

Zuki instructed the keepers of the alien to give it the necessary amount of food and drink to keep it healthy, remove the hand shackles and give it bed to lie on – but to keep an eye on it, in case it tried to escape.

As they left the interrogation room, Kono said to Zuki:

'You know, 'ol Brond gets a bit tetchy sometimes, I wonder why?'

'Well, I wouldn't say he was out of his depth,' Zuki answered, 'but he's a bit near the edge sometimes, as we all are. The possible threat of another attack, and the chance that we may be able to develop interstellar flight from the crashed alien ship – if we get it right - and don't lose our alien in the meantime. It's enough to make anyone a bit edgy.'

'Hmmm,' said Kono.

With nothing else on the agenda at the moment, the pair boarded a transport and headed out to the alien crash site. As they were about to enter the craft, a high-ranking officer barred their way.

'And just who are you?' he enquired discourteously.

'He's in charge of this whole project,' replied Kono, drawing himself up to his full height, 'and stand to attention when you address him.'

Later Zuki told Kono he didn't really have to do that, to which Kono replied,

'I didn't like his attitude. Anyway, he's too stuffed up with his own self importance.'

Zuki tried to suppress the little chuckle which bubbled up. It was nice to know he had a defender.

Several of the floor plates had been removed, and peering down to the depths below, they could see two engineers making notes and sketches of what they had found.

'Can one of you come up, and brief me on what you have found please?' asked Zuki.

The man scrambled up the ladder, with a big grin on his face.

'We're in luck,' he said, getting his breath back, 'the whole thing is composed of plug-in modules. This means we can dismantle it, and reassemble it back at the complex. There's only one problem, we've not found out how to start the dammed thing up. Have you got any ideas?'

'I'm not sure,' said Zuki, 'but I think it may be controlled by the pilot, so that means from the units we have assembled back at base, the ones which control the visuals. Have you found the drive units yet?'

'We know where they are,' replied the engineer, 'by tracing the power leads. But so far, we haven't got to them – shouldn't take too long now.'

It took several days for the two power units to be dismantled, along with the main drive engines, all being shipped back to the complex. It took even longer for the engineers to figure out what did what, and then they held a debriefing in the canteen.

The chief engineer stood up, cleared his throat twice, and began.

'We have duplicated the pilot's controls with our own components and got it working. The two power units have been dismantled, and we have figured out how most of it works, except for the torus, of which there are two. They seem to be made of some alloy we have no knowledge of, but we are working on that too. Once we can find out what that is, we should be able to duplicate it. Once that is done, we should have a working space drive. We can't be certain, but we think the drive unit generates some sort of energy field which engulfs the whole ship. But how it moves it, we don't know as of yet. Any questions?'

There was stunned silence for several minutes, and then a somewhat shaky hand went up – and then wished it hadn't.

'If you power the whole thing up, won't it just disappear off into space?'

The resulting laughter defused the tension, and several sensible questions followed, illustrating that most present had grasped the situation and what it implied quite well.

After the meeting, Brond announced to Zuki and Kono that there was little for them to do until the engineers had finished their work. They should take some leave and they would be recalled when needed. The alien had recovered from its starvation regime, and seemed to be in good health. Brond was, if nothing else, a very good organiser, and kept the necessary information flowing to the correct terminals.

Kono was again invited back to Zuki's home; his parents having got used to him from the last visit – all fear of their minds being 'blown' having diminished.

Zuki was authorised to tell them the bare outlines of what had occurred during his absence, but the finer details would have to remain a secret for a little longer.

Once a couple of days relaxing had passed, Kono and Zuki got restless and sought out the city's record office. Under the pretence of looking for data about the first lot of aliens to attack their system, they were really interested in any information about the strange crystals that used to be mined near his old home, and which both had experienced.

Once the personnel of the records office had got used to their presence, they were left alone to do their research unhindered, which was what they needed.

Information about the crystals seemed very general - just that they were considered very valuable, and needed special handling. There was no mention of what they were used for, where they were sent, or who wanted them.

'I think there is a lot more data about them here somewhere.' said Zuki, 'There must be – they were so important.'

'Ask one or two of the archive keepers if there is,' Kono offered, 'and I'll try to pick up any resistance to your question. That should tell us if it exists and is worth pursuing.'

The third archivist came up trumps, without knowing it.

'He knows something.' said Kono, 'It's something in some old wooden cabinets, but I couldn't get a clear picture of where it is.'

'Well,' said Zuki, 'let's have a casual wander about, they can't be that hard to find.'

On the second day of their 'wanderings', they found three old wooden cabinets. Pretending to be very interested in local farming practises, they waited until all personnel had vacated the room, and then began their search. The first few folders only contained generalities, but then they found what they were looking for.

Kono had brought along a small camera, and the relevant pages were copied to read at their leisure. The pair thanked everyone for their help, and left, saying they might be back at some time in the future.

They rushed back to Zuki's parent's home, ate their evening meal with indecent haste, and retired to Zuki's room.

Printing out the pages large enough for comfortable reading took up most of the evening, and then they sat down to read the 'forbidden' details about the crystals.

It transpired that someone from one of the mountain tribes had chanced upon one of the crystals a very long time ago, and had been affected. Someone else noticed the difference in the finder, and reported it to someone in higher authority. The 'masters' then got involved, and the finder was then interviewed and his enhanced abilities checked out. It was obvious the crystal had affected the man, and so the search for more crystals began.

At this time, the populace had already diverged into two separate types – those who wanted to advance through science, and those who considered such a practice was 'against nature', and took themselves off to become the 'mountain tribes', (which exist to this day.)

A mountain tribe was persuaded to begin mining the mountain where the man had had his strange experience, but when a crystal was found, it affected the finder.

The scientists then devised a means of collecting the crystals in a box-like construction. When a crystal was found, the finder immediately withdrew and a scientist was called, the crystal was collected, and quickly whisked away to the city.

Over time, selected scientists and high officials were exposed to a crystal which greatly enhanced their abilities, but the practice was confined to a select few – and the knowledge withheld from the public.

Eventually, they could find no more crystals, despite a thorough search, and the miners returned to their homes, and the whole crystal incident was lost in the mists of time.

'How long ago did this happen?' asked Kono.

'I don't know,' Zuki replied, 'the dating system on these papers isn't like that which we use today, so I can't work it out. I would think it happened a very long time ago.'

'I don't understand the collecting box thing.' said Kono, 'What's that all about?'

'I'm not too sure,' Zuki replied, 'but I remember when my brushwood torch lit up the crystal and it seemed to get brighter. My torch went out, but the crystal seemed to glow even brighter, it drew something from me, and I passed out. When I recovered, I couldn't see the crystal – it was pitch black – and then I saw a glimmer of light from the tunnel I had come in by, and crawled down it to my sleeping cave.'

'But what about the box thing they used,' asked Kono, 'I still don't understand that.'

'I think it takes a little time for the crystal to pick up something from the finder,' Zuki replied, 'so if you withdraw at once, the crystal can't lock on to you, so to speak. That's when the scientist comes in with the box thing, quickly collects the crystal, keeping it in the dark – it then can't connect to anyone.'

Kono paused for a moment, deep in thought.

'I don't understand why we gain these abilities after seeing the crystal,' said Kono, 'it's only a piece of crystal.'

'I think it's a bit more than that,' Zuki replied, 'I don't understand it either, but it's just possible it's some form of life force locked in the crystal. When it is lit up and someone looks at it, it somehow joins with us – maybe our increased abilities are a sort of gift from it, for releasing it from the crystal. That's how I see it, anyway.' He added.

They pawed over the papers they had printed out until the early hours of next day, but were none the wiser for their efforts.

After a hurried breakfast, Zuki took his adoptive father to one side, and told him what they had been doing.

'Well, that explains a few things,' his father said, 'I knew there was something different about you, but couldn't quite figure it out. So that's why Brond and his outfit were so keen for you to join them. Yes, it all fits together now. I suppose you will be going back to him?'

'Yes,' Zuki said, 'there is still a lot to do. I can't tell you what the next phase is just yet, but we must prepare ourselves, in case another lot of aliens come to find out what happened to the first lot. All I can say now is that we stand a good chance of handling them, if they do come.'

Several weeks went by, and Zuki and Kono were getting itchy feet. They were missing the excitement and buzz of the complex, and then came the call from Brond to return at once.

'Well?' asked Zuki when they met up, 'What's been happening during our absence?' He asked cheerily.

'Quite a lot,' Brond replied, 'we've analysed their weapons, and from the data we got have improved ours. After a bit of a struggle, we've found out what the torus ring is made of, duplicated it, and fired it up – it works, and how! You wouldn't believe the power it gives out. A ship's hull has been sent up into orbit, a copy of the alien's drive unit fitted, and they are now sending up two duplicated power units. When that lot is finally assembled, we'll be ready to try it out.'

'I can't wait to have a go at that,' exclaimed Zuki, 'that's beyond my wildest dreams.'

'Sorry son, we can't let you go on the test flight – you're far too valuable here. Once everything is tested and proved safe, well, we'll see.'

To say Zuki was disappointed was a severe understatement.

'Look, I'm sorry,' said Brond, 'I have my orders, and it's for the good of all. You might like to see one thing we've developed. It's a laser cannon – got the idea from one of the alien's weapons, and modified it. Let's go out to the firing range, I'd like you to see it.'

The three of them boarded a transport and flew out to where the testing was done – a deep valley surrounded by mountains.

In the far distance, a massive wall of black rock rose up vertically to meet the sky, its surface pitted with deep holes. They walked up to an eight wheeled flatbed truck, on which was mounted one of the duplicated power units. At the front end of the truck, a small cabin with a short stubby barrel protruding out pointed at the far distant rock face.

'Now this you can have a go at,' said Brond, 'and I don't think you'll be disappointed. Just take a seat, line up the sights at that rock face, and press the button.'

Zuki sat down, wriggled to get comfortable, lined up the sights, and pressed the button.

For a moment there was a deep hum, a slight shudder of the cabin, and a section of the rock face disintegrated in a cloud of dust and a flash of light.

'We haven't been out to measure it,' said Brond, 'but from here we estimate those holes are about five metres across, and about as deep. Were not quite sure yet, but it seems to be some sort of disrupter beam. It sort of breaks the molecular bonds of the rock, and all you see is very fine dust, almost like a mist.'

The dust cloud slowly drifted upwards, then dispersed in the light winds which blew across the top of the mountains, and there was another hole in the rock face.

'That is far more powerful than anything we have right now,' said Brond, 'and I don't think we've pushed it to its limits. If the aliens come again, they'll be in for a nasty surprise. I don't think their weapons are as powerful as this thing.' He added, patting the stubby barrel.

Although Zuki was impressed by the power of the weapon, not being on the test flight of their new spaceship was still niggling at him, and Brond could see it.

'Have a look at this,' he said, 'it's another development from an idea taken from the alien's weapons. We call it a stun gun. It doesn't kill, but you are paralysed if hit by it. It sort of overloads your nervous system, and you can't move.'

Zuki took the weapon from Brond, and turned it over in his hands.

'Just point it at that goat, and press the button.' said Brond, 'Don't look so worried, we've zapped the poor little sod several times, and it doesn't seem any the worse for it.'

Zuki pointed the gun at the goat, pressed the button, and the goat just dropped to the ground, as though it was asleep.

'You'd have a job to beat that for close combat,' said Brond brightly, trying to cheer Zuki up – but it didn't work.

They boarded the transport and returned to the complex to be greeted by one of the men who looked after the aliens from the carrier ships.

'I'm sorry, sir,' he said, 'but it looks as if one of them has died. Its body is stone cold and as stiff as a board. We found it this morning, lying on the canteen floor. I don't know how it got out of its holding quarters – but it did – somehow.'

All three of them rushed to the canteen to see just what had happened. The body of the alien lay next to one of the tables, the remains of a sugar-coated bun by its side.

'The silly sod's been eating our food,' exclaimed Brond, 'I bet it's the sugar that caused the problem. Someone check to see if their food contains sugar – and quickly.'

The Attendant rushed off, and was soon back with the news that the alien's food didn't contain sugar, but did contain some carbohydrates.

'Right, thanks for that.' said Brond, 'Please tell the other attendants 'nothing for the aliens with a sugar content'. Oh, and tighten up security – we can't have 'em running about all over the place. And please arrange for the body to be taken away for autopsy, we may learn something from it.'

'How about the other alien, the one from the attack ship?' asked Zuki, 'How about we question him a little more? He seemed to have given up the tight lip routine.'

'Good idea,' said Brond, 'let's do it now.'

The linguists, working with the carrier aliens, had increased the size of the code sheet considerably, making it much easier to formulate questions to the alien.

The three of them sat down in the interrogation room, and the alien was brought in. Its hands were free, but the foot shackles were still in place.

'Are you getting enough food and drink?' asked Zuki.

'Yes.' came back, through the translator.

'We regret we are unable to send you to your home world, but all your ships are destroyed, and our ships would not go that far.' It was a long sentence, and Zuki hoped the translator would be able to cope. There was a long pause before it did.

'I miss my people.' was the reply.

'We have some from the carrier ships,' Zuki said, 'you could see some of them.'

'Not my people.' came back.

'Fussy little sod,' Brond muttered, 'they seem a decent lot compared to him.'

'Will others come here?' asked Zuki.

'Not from my people. They will think we go on looking for the minerals.'

'We could have given you the minerals.' Zuki said.

'I know now.' came back.

'Didn't say sorry, did he?' Brond added, 'Perhaps it's not in his vocabulary.'

'We will look after you,' Zuki offered, 'until we can return you.'

'Your ships no good.' came back.

'They may be one day.' Zuki added, not wishing to give anything away. The alien just shrugged.

'If we return you, will we be attacked?' asked Zuki.

'Most likely.' was the reply.

'What we need is one of their engineers.' said Brond, 'This one is a bit short on technicalities.'

'Not much hope of that,' said Zuki, 'if there was one on board, it's long gone now. This one is the only survivor, and it was piloting the ship. I very much doubt it has any tech knowledge.'

The alien was taken away, its foot shackles rattling, letting it know it was not trusted fully.

'What's next on the agenda?' asked Zuki.

'We are waiting for the final touches to be done on our test ship. If that works, the universe is ours.' Brond said, sounding satisfied with proceedings so far.

'I wouldn't bank on that,' Zuki said, 'just how many more races are there out there?'

Two days passed before the test ship was ready for its first flight, and although there was no certainty that it would be a safe journey, there were no shortages of volunteers for the task of putting it through its paces.

'We'll watch it from here on a relay from the space station.' said Brond, 'It's too risky to be up there until we know for sure it's safe.'

'What about the poor devils who are doing the test?' Zuki asked.

'They volunteered,' Brond responded, 'and know the risks. If all goes well, they will be suitably rewarded.'

'He's a lot harder than I thought.' Zuki said in an aside to Kono.

'No, he isn't,' Kono replied, 'he feels the same way we do – he's just being practical. I picked that up from him.'

They all piled into Brond's room, where a relay screen had been set up and a clear picture of the test ship shimmering in the light from the sun filled the screen.

'It looks like one of our ordinary ships,' Kono said.

'That's because it is,' Brond responded, 'it's a standard hull, but with the new drive unit fitted. A small space tug will move it out from the space station, as we don't know if the field it generates might take a piece of the station with it if they are too close.'

A small tug appeared to one side of the screen, a space suited figure drifted across to the test ship, attached a towing cable, and returned to the tug.

Slowly the test ship was moved out about two thousand metres from its mooring position on the space station, and the towing cable removed. The tug then moved off to one side.

A voice came over the sound system, 'Stand by to launch on my count......three, two, one, launch.' The test ship seemed to shimmer slightly, as though a hazy film had passed over it, and then it moved. Slowly at first, but then it accelerated, quickly becoming a tiny dot of light in the far distance – and then it was gone.

'My God,' commented Kono, 'those poor devils in there must be flattened by now with that acceleration.'

'Oh, come on Kono, haven't you been listening? The drive field encompasses the whole ship, and everything in it – they all move at the same time.'

'Well, it seems to work,' Zuki added, 'how far will they go?'

'About half a parsec from our system, and then return,' Brond answered, 'that should prove its stability. We'll have to attach one of our drive units to it for manoeuvring. We can't have a someone going out with a tow cable every time for local manoeuvring.'

'With a small fleet of those ships fitted with that new laser cannon,' Zuki said, 'we should be able to look after ourselves, come what may.'

Some twenty minutes later, a voice announced that the ship had been picked up on the long-distance detectors, and then it came into view – a tiny dot of light which quickly grew in size until it was recognisable as the ship.

'Right, everyone down to the debriefing room,' said Brond, 'I want to hear what they have to say first hand.'

There were about fifty people in the debriefing room, all loudly voicing their opinions about the flight, and after what appeared to be a long wait, a door opened on the back of the stage and silence fell like a heavy blanket as the pilot and crew entered.

As the crew sat down at the long table on the stage, a rousing cheer threatened to shatter the light tubes in the ceiling, and then there was silence again as the captain of the ship stood up.

'I am very pleased to say the flight went exactly as planned – well done to the engineers who set her up. We set co-ordinates for a run of half a parsec into clear space of about two parsecs, decelerated, swept around in an arc, and reset for home. One thing we didn't expect was that at about light speed, the stars disappeared – it was just blackness. I must admit we were a bit concerned at this, as we have never experienced that before – but we have never travelled at that speed before.'

A nervous ripple of laughter ran through the room.

'I would only make one suggestion, whoever made the controls based on the alien ship, failed to mark the velocity indicator in our language! So we have no idea of what speed we obtained. Apart from that, a very big 'well done' to those who built her.'

Thunderous applause and cheering went on for some time after the crew had left, and Brond got up to go.

'I know it's a great achievement, but any more of that, and I'll have to have my ear drums replaced.'

'It's a bit of an anticlimax,' Zuki said, at their midday meal break, 'after all the excitement and rushing around. So what's next Brond?'

'We have to build a defence fleet,' Brond replied, 'and we have a bunch of tame aliens on our hands, and one who is a bit doubtful about its intentions. It seems a bit more co-operative now, but I wouldn't trust it somehow. Were you serious about sending it back to its home world, Zuki?'

'We have the means now, so it's a possibility.' Zuki replied, 'I don't think we'll get anything more useful from it. We could set it up with its own secure compound and let it live out its natural life, I suppose. I somehow don't like the idea of just killing it, and the others.' Brond just grunted.

'I wonder just how much more life there is out there in the universe?' asked Kono, 'I know this was the first encounter we've had, but surely there must be more.'

'Don't doubt it for a moment,' said Brond, 'but I don't think we should advertise our existence just yet, until we can handle anything we may come across.'

The old mining camps on the outermost planet of the system were opened up again, as the minerals were needed for the manufacture of the new power plants. The construction of a small fleet of the new ships, complete with the laser cannon got underway. But it would be some time before they were ready for use, hence Brond's insistence that their prototype ship didn't leave their system until it too had been fitted with the laser weapon, to defend itself if necessary – and then only when the new fleet was nearly ready.

Zuki decided, with Brond's permission, to visit the aliens from the carrier fleet to see if he could glean any more information about their home world. Armed with the new translation sheets, he felt he could have a near normal conversation with them, as they seemed co-operative.

From what he could gather, most of the population were like those he was interviewing, while a small elite group ran their world. The aliens in the attack ships were something else. It would seem that they were specially bred for their aggressive and fearless qualities, with a total lack of fear for their own wellbeing when on a mission. Fortunately, there were not too many of them, so the threat of a future attack diminished somewhat.

Zuki found his interviewees mainly a peaceful and pleasant lot, and he wondered if they too had been specially bred for ease of control, and later relayed all this information on to Brond.

A thought kept returning to Zuki's mind. What if the aliens on the eleven attack ships had not all been killed – perhaps a few just stunned? Could they return to the attack? He consulted Brond on the matter, and he immediately ordered the long-range detectors to be set up to scan the area in which the aliens had last been seen.

While examining the weapons and other items from the crashed alien ship, several new ideas were sparked off, resulting in new weapons and other gadgets which kept Zuki and Kono entertained for some time. They watched the trials, and sometimes actually tried them out. One of which was a smaller version of the laser cannon, with different controls. This proved useful for mining, as it just gently disintegrated the material where the beam struck, making it easier to remove the debris in the form of fine gravel.

Brond suggested that Zuki and Kono took some more leave to recover from the tensions of the past few days, and they did so. Brond also told them they could tell Zuki's parents the basic outlines of what they had been doing, but the details were not to be related.

The pair had been home for a couple of days when they had a visitor.

The chief archivist of long ago whom Zuki had visited with his adoptive father was standing there, and asked if he may come in.

When all were seated, he began.

'I remember you were very interested in the old mines in the Out Lands, and the crystals that were found there. Are you still interested?'

'Yes, to some degree,' Zuki replied warily.

'We have searched the whole archive for more data, but found none,' the archivist said, 'and we wondered if you had?'

'Nothing very much,' Zuki replied, knowing the man was lying. He would now have to be very careful what he said – someone had a little more than a healthy interest in the crystals, and him.

'Well, what have you found out?' the man asked, looking intently at Zuki.

'I've asked several people about them,' Zuki replied, 'but most have never heard of them, and those who did only knew that they might have existed at some time in the distant past. Why are you so interested in something which only exists in folklore?'

'What do you know of the old mines, where you used to live?' asked the man.

'I didn't know there were any,' said Zuki, 'no one has ever mentioned them to me.'

There was a long pause.

'What would you do if you found a crystal?' asked the man.

'I don't know,' said Zuki, 'what is one supposed to do?'

'If you did find one, we could add it to the archive.' The man said.

'What, that old piece of paper you showed us? What use would that be, no one is interested in those old tales, are they?'

The archivist was getting frustrated. He sensed Zuki knew something, but couldn't formulate a question which would extract the information.

'I shall have to take this to someone in higher authority. It's an offence to withhold information which might be useful to us.'

'Now that's interesting,' Zuki retorted, 'just who is 'us'? I thought you were just the chief archivist.'

'You will hear from us again.' The man said, and got up to leave.

Zuki saw him to the door and said, 'If I find a crystal, I'll bring it to you. But don't hold your breath.'

Chapter 8
The Next Phase

'WHAT THE HELL was that all about?' asked Kono, 'A bit officious, I thought.'

'I don't know, but I don't like it.' replied Zuki, 'Either someone is good at guessing, or our little secret has leaked out. Brond only thinks I am a little smarter than average, and he knows you have the mind thing. So where's this coming from?'

'If you get any more pressure,' Kono suggested, 'I'd have a word with Brond. He should be able to put a clamp on it.'

The unpleasant incident was passed, but was not forgotten.

The pair spent the next few days in the 'museum of antiquities', which was a huge building containing samples of their progress through the ages. Zuki was interested in the points in time when great inventions and progress had appeared, as he felt sure that was when a crystal had enhanced someone's abilities well above normal.

'As far as I can make out,' said Zuki, 'it all started about three or four hundred years ago. There were several big scientific breakthroughs, and the old system of politics with opposing parties was done away with – replaced with people voting for a representative for each region. If the guy didn't do his job well enough, he was voted out and replaced with someone who could. Opposing parties in a government just put the brakes on progress.'

'But there's no mention of the crystals,' said Kono, 'I'd have thought they would have got a mention – just look at what has been achieved with them.'

'I think it was a closely guarded secret among those in charge.' said Zuki, 'Certain people being chosen for the treatment where necessary. Until the crystals ran out, and then it was all hushed up, for some reason.'

'Think we'll ever really know for sure?' asked Kono

'Well, we know about the crystals and how they work,' Zuki replied, 'and I think we should keep it strictly to ourselves for the time being. Such information should only be released into a society which is very stable, otherwise all sorts of troubles could arise.'

The pair went over the printouts of the old documents they had copied from the archives, just to make sure they hadn't missed anything important, but nothing new was discovered.

A couple of days later, and Brond requested their recall to the complex.

'Looks like we may have a problem.' he greeted them with, 'We've picked up an object on a direct course for us. Can't say what it is at the moment, could be an asteroid or a big ship. Two of our new ships equipped with laser canons have been completed. You two want to get involved in the action?' he asked.

'You bet,' said Kono, while Zuki just nodded.

'As soon as I have any more data, I'll let you know.' said Brond, 'Don't stray too far away, we may need you in a hurry.'

Zuki and Kono hurried off to the canteen, not knowing when they would get another decent meal; they had barely finished, when Brond was back.

'Just heard from the detector crew, they feel pretty certain it's an asteroid, so we'll send both ships out and hope that will be enough power to blow it apart.'

'They'll have to reduce it to dust to be effective.' said Zuki, 'Just breaking it up will mean the pieces will still hit us, and do a lot of damage. Are we allowed to go?' he asked.

'Yes, you can,' Brond replied, 'but you couldn't if it had been a ship – OK?'

All three rushed out to shuttle and were soon on their way up to the space station where the two new ships were. Transfer to the ships completed, they began the journey to the outer fringe of their system to meet the incoming asteroid. With the new drive units, they had no problem in meeting it just outside their system, and lined up to deliver their first blows to the invader.

'It's no use just banging away at it,' said Zuki, 'you'll have to systematically disintegrate it from one end through to the other. Not chop it into pieces, or we'll have real rouble.'

Brond quickly gave orders for both ships to attack the front end of the asteroid, making sure no large pieces were left to travel on to their home world.

The ships manoeuvred to what they considered to be a safe distance from the asteroid, matched speed and then turned to face it, and began the attack.

Huge clouds of fine particles billowed out from the front end of the asteroid as the lasers did their work, everyone hoping the power units could keep up the huge flow of energy needed.

The two ships had just passed the orbit of the mining planet when the order to cease fire was given, as the detectors didn't register any more pieces of the asteroid big enough to cause much damage if their world was hit.

An enormous cloud of dust particles was now heading in towards the centre of the system, at worst it would only rain down on their world as fine particles. Most likely it would burn up in the atmosphere, as it still was travelling at high velocity.

'Well, you've seen what those lasers can do,' said Brond, 'so what do you think?'

'If the aliens knew we had that sort of firepower,' said Kono, 'I doubt they'd have come within a couple of parsecs of us. But in a way, it's just as well they did, or we wouldn't have the new lasers or the power supplies for them.'

'It cost a lot of lives,' Zuki added, 'but in a purely practical point of view, it was worth it. Unless someone has something bigger and better, we are invincible.'

Both ships turned and headed back to the space station, their first trial having been a great success. The trio were keen to get back to the complex so they could witness any effects the particle cloud might have if it hit their world, missing the party the space station had ready for them.

As they entered the complex, they were greeted by hand claps and cheers from the assembled staff who were able to leave their stations – and then they had their party.

Several days later, part of the cloud hit. The night sky was lit up almost like daylight, and the worry now was just how much oxygen had been burnt up in the process. Brond immediately ordered samples of air to be checked for the next few days, although there was not much anyone could do about it if it had been depleted.

The following day, Zuki took Brond to one side and told him about the archivist who had been harassing him.

'Do you know why he is doing that?' asked Brond.

'Sort of,' Zuki replied, 'I'd rather not give you the details, if that's all right with you. I just want him off my back.'

'OK, I can see to that,' Brond said, 'you needn't worry about him anymore.'

Two more of the carrier aliens had now died, but no one was sure just why. The alien from the attacking ship had settled down in its compound – seemingly quite contented, but being so alien, no one was really sure of that either.

The rest of the asteroid dust cloud passed the planet by harmlessly, admittedly obscuring the sunlight for a while, and the oxygen tests proved that no lasting damage had been done to the atmosphere.

By the end of the week, two more of the new spaceships had been completed and tested. Just two more, and they would have a formidable fleet to protect themselves with, that's if any more aliens decided to visit and be aggressive.

Zuki and Kono were enjoying themselves again in the 'Antiquities Museum', when they were interrupted yet again.

Brond sent a message: 'Come back to the complex soonest. I need to see you both.'

'Now what's gone wrong?' said Kono, 'Thought everything was a bit quiet.'

Zuki didn't say anything. Although he had an instinctive guess as to what it was likely to be, he didn't want to say anything in case he was wrong.

As soon as they entered the complex, a uniformed man met them and said, 'Follow me please,' in a very business like manner. They were soon ushered into Brond's office, and this time he didn't rise to greet them.

'Something has come up,' he said, with a stern look on his face, 'and I need some answers from you two.'

The pair looked at each other, Kono shrugged, and then they looked back at Brond expectantly.

'This is really serious,' Brond said, 'and I don't want any evasions or half truths. There is a little more to you two than meets the eye, and someone very high up has spotted it, and wants some answers – which I was unable to give.'

'Have we done something wrong?' asked Zuki.

'It's not what you've done,' Brond replied, 'it's what you are. I knew you, Zuki, were different to anyone else I'd ever met, and you had abilities we desperately needed. We used those abilities to get us out of trouble, and it worked – no fault there, and we're grateful for your contributions in sorting out the alien threat. But someone has spotted that difference, and wants to know how you acquired it, and I was unable to tell them.'

'Surely every now and then,' Zuki replied, 'someone is going to turn up with different abilities from the norm. I don't see anything wrong with that.'

'I said no evasions,' Brond said sternly, 'and that was one.'

'OK, what is it exactly that you want to know?' asked Zuki.

'You belonged to a tribe of low intelligent misfits, scraping a living in the outer lands, just about surviving. You were rescued, joined a family of our people, and changed. Just being a little brighter would have gone unnoticed, but you were different. Before we got you to join us, we checked your academic abilities, and they were way ahead of any on record. I did wonder at the time how this could be, but we needed someone like you – we were desperate. The only explanation I can think of is that something happened to you between your tribe being wiped out, and your early school days. I want to know what it was.'

'If I told you,' said Zuki, 'you probably wouldn't believe me. I can only just make sense of it myself.'

'Try me.' Brond said patiently, 'Not only were you very bright, but you managed to do something we couldn't do, and that was contact Kono, and somehow tame his mind blast. Just how the hell did you do that?'

'I didn't tame Kono's mind blast, he did that himself,' Zuki blurted out.

'Well, he couldn't do that before he met you.' Brond said firmly, 'So, what happened between you two?'

Zuki knew Brond wouldn't give up until he had the whole story, no matter how hard he tried to evade revealing what he knew about the crystals. So he told him, in great detail, including the copied papers from the archive, and then how Kono also had the same experience in the cave on his world. Brond sat back in his chair, his face set, and without a smile.

'I thought it might be something like that – but the crystal thing is a surprise. As far as we know, no crystals have been found for many generations. Your abilities have struck a chord with someone well above my rank, and they recognised something. I think they must have some knowledge of the crystals, and they're keen to find them.'

'Don't see how we can help,' Zuki said, 'we found them by accident. We weren't looking for them - didn't even know they existed until it happened.'

'Well, I'll relay back what you've told me, but you can expect a bit of pressure from now on. Those crystals are very much sought after, and they won't give up until they find them. One thing which began the whole ball rolling was your poking about in the archives. Anything out of the ordinary gets picked up by someone – and you two certainly fit that category.'

'So, what happens now?' asked Kono, 'We've done our bit – helped you lot all we can, so why can't they leave us alone to get on with life?'

'You don't seem to realise just how valuable those crystals are,' Brond came back with, 'try to realise what they've done to you two, and then what they could do for others.'

'The only thing we can do is recognise them when we see them. But anyone can do that, so why are we involved?' asked Zuki.

'I don't think the 'powers that be' fully understand the situation.' Brond replied, 'They just want the crystals. They would, I would suspect, stop at nothing to get them.'

'Don't forget,' Kono added firmly, 'I can defend myself, and that goes for Zuki too.'

'Come on men, don't let's get into threats,' Brond said, 'there's no need for that. I will do all I can to smooth things over. Just be aware that these things are above any value you can put on them - and someone wants them. Once I've explained the situation, they may see a little reason.'

'I hope they do, for their sake,' Kono said, driving home the point, 'my so-called human brothers have given me a raw deal so far, through no fault of my own. I shan't forget that.'

The meeting came to an end, with Brond telling them to 'keep a low profile'. But they were at a loss as to how they could achieve that, bearing in mind that everyone knew them, and what they had done.

Although they met up with Brond several times over the next few days, nothing was said about the incident. They had almost forgotten about it, when they had a visit from two very smartly uniformed men.

'We represent the High Counsel,' one of them said, 'and we would like you both to accompany us to the city.'

'What for?' asked Zuki.

'We have not been privileged with that information,' the man replied, 'just to locate you, and escort you to the city. Will you comply?'

'And what if we don't?' said an infuriated Kono, 'Bearing in mind what I can do.'

'We sincerely hope it won't come to that,' the man replied with a smile, 'will you comply?'

'I don't think we have an option, really,' Zuki said to Kono, 'I don't see any harm in talking to someone – a long as that's all there is to it.'

Kono looked sullen for a moment, and then reluctantly agreed.

A transport whisked them on their way, the high spires of the city coming into view sooner than they expected.

'God, this thing is certainly fast,' said Zuki.

'It is one of the fastest we have,' one of the escort men said, 'although I've heard they are working on something even faster.'

The transport swooped down in a smooth curve to land on the top of one of the spires.

A short journey in a very plush lift, and they were faced with a massive dark wooden door, one of the escorts discreetly knocked on it.

'Yes?' came from a sound unit somewhere above them, and the man replied,

'We have the two gentlemen you wished to speak to, sir.'

The doors silently opened, and before them was an equally plush room, a large desk, and an elderly man seated behind it. He smiled.

'Please come in and take a seat, gentlemen. Would you like some refreshments?'

'Not at the moment, thank you,' said a wary Zuki.

'My name is Gleeson.' the man said, still smiling, 'Please, take a seat, we have much to talk about.'

The pair sat down, the seats adjusting themselves for their maximum comfort, Gleeson smiled again at the surprised look on their faces.

'First of all,' said Gleeson, 'I would like to thank you both, on behalf of countless million of our grateful citizens who will never have the chance to do so, for your co-operation and knowledge which has helped us repel the alien's invasion. It is doubtful if there would be much of our world left, if it had not been for you two. I think we might have won, but the cost would have been enormous.'

The pair nodded their heads, not quite knowing what to say.

'And now to the matter in hand.' said Gleeson, 'We understand you have both experienced the effect the crystals can have on a person. One of my men has found the same data you did in the archives, so I am up to speed regarding the data on these extraordinary things. We too have realised that our sciences, and other things too, have been advanced in the past through contact with them, and we would like to continue this advancement. But we have a problem – there appears to be no more crystals available. And yet you two found some. My question is this, would you both be willing help us to find any which have escaped our most thorough searches?'

'We don't mind helping you,' said Zuki, 'but we came upon them by accident. We weren't looking for them. In fact, we didn't even know they existed until it happened, so how can we help you?'

'We know the original crystals came from the mountains where you used to live, Zuki. All we ask is that you use whatever skills you have between you, to find any that were missed.'

'That seems reasonable,' Zuki said, 'what say you, Kono?'

Kono thought for a moment, 'I don't much like crawling about in tunnels,' he said.

'We have people who are expert at tunnelling, so you won't have to do anything you do not wish to do. All we ask is that you help us, where you can.' Kono nodded his head.

Gleeson's eyebrows raised slightly as he looked at Zuki.

'I don't see how we can say no.' Zuki responded, looking at Kono, who nodded, 'We have finished all the projects we were working on, and this would be something different. OK, we'll do it.'

'Thank you both,' said Gleeson, 'I want you both to realise we would not have used force, or any kind of coercion, if you had refused. I'll get in touch with Brond to make the necessary arrangements; I understand he is a very good friend of yours.'

'Well, he's our boss,' Kono said, and then realised he probably was their friend, really.

The next day Brond paid them a visit, a big smile on his face.

'Looks like we're going to have another adventure.' he said, 'Perhaps not quite so much pressure or buzz, but it could be exciting.'

He certainly got that right...

Part 3
Power
Released

Chapter 9
The Expedition

With Zuki and Kono, Brond called a meeting comprising three top officials of the Counsel, who had been allocated to the job of sanctioning a mission to the Outlands.

'Gentlemen,' he began, 'I seek your agreement to run an operation in secret to the Outlands. Something has been discovered that I think might be of great benefit to our society, but I can't release details of it yet. It is known that a certain section of the Council has an operations unit devoted to picking up anything unusual. I must insist that they do not probe into our operation – if they do, I'll close it down, and destroy any data we may have gained. That is how important this operation is. Do I have your total agreement?'

The three Council members muttered among themselves for a moment.

'We do not think you have the authority to demand such conditions, and we don't think they are necessary in the first place. What say you?'

'My authority to run this operation comes straight from the Chief Councillor,' Brond said, in a very steady voice, 'with all due respects, I don't think you have the faintest idea what this mission is all about, and I am not authorised to tell you in any detail. Quite frankly, I don't even know why you have been chosen to be in this meeting – especially as you obviously haven't been briefed on the situation. I must have your complete co-operation on this matter, or you can take it up with the Chief Councillor.'

To say the three councillors looked stunned, would be an understatement. All three looked a bit pink around the gills and muttered in low tones among themselves for several minutes.

'We will agree, if you can prove your orders came from the Chief Councillor,' one of them said, 'and only then.'

Brond pushed a red sealed document towards them and sat back with a look of certainty on his face.

'Having seen this, of course we agree.' one of them said, 'We will ensure no one interferes or intrudes on this operation. Until now, we didn't understand its importance. Is there anything else we can implement to comply with your wishes?'

'No, gentlemen,' said Brond, 'that is all I require. This operation is going to be difficult enough, without certain personnel sticking their noses in, if you see what I mean. Thank you.'

With that, the three councillors got up and left, a little more contrite than when they came in.

'My God,' said Zuki, 'that was a bit strong.'

'Although this world runs quite well,' Brond replied, 'it's only due to a few bright councillors in the right places. But there are many posts to fill, and not enough bright ones to fill them. That was a good example of the 'not so bright brigade'.'

Kono opened his mouth to say something, thought about it, and then clamped it shut.

'What I propose,' began Brond, 'and I would like your opinion on it, is that we make up a team of you two, me, a geologist and a mineralogist, to try and locate the old mines. If we find them, we can bring in a team of tunnellers, and begin our search. The geologist will be able to classify the type of strata, so we can look for any other occurrences of it. The mineralogist will be able to recognise the type of rock we need to search in – that's if we find the old mines in the first place. If that works, we'll bring in some prefab buildings for us all to live in, while we do the search. There's only one problem. We don't know about the construction of the holding box, if we find any crystals.'

'What about the little tribes which inhabit the foot of the mountain?' asked Zuki, 'They could be a bit of a nuisance – some are darned right aggressive, like the ones which wiped out my village. I don't think it would be a good idea to have troops to guard us, it would bring too much attention to what we are doing.'

'I think we should be able to look after ourselves.' Brond replied, 'I have just received the latest stun device from the research lab. It's like the one you tried, but much smaller. You could have it in your pocket with your finger on the button, and then point the other arm at the aggressor. Press the button and it will give the impression of some sort of superpower – that should quell any over-ambitious attacker, especially when word gets around.'

'Got to give it to you, Brond, you seem to be one step ahead, most of the time.' said Kono. Brond tried to hide the smile which flickered across his face.

'What about accommodation?' Zuki enquired.

'We can use one of the big transports,' Brond replied, 'I can arrange to have bunks fitted in the cargo hold, and a small kitchen, any other ideas?'

'You should go up the ranks a bit, Brond,' Kono said, 'that's if we pull it off.'

'I'll make sure we all do,' Brond replied.

The transport was fitted out to Brond's instructions, and sent on its way to Zuki's old village – as good a starting point as any, Brond thought.

Three days leave at Zuki's parent's home, and Brond sent word that they were ready to leave.

He introduced the mineralogist and geologist to Zuki and Kono, and the team got aboard the transport. It gracefully soared up into the clear morning air and headed out over the rolling sands of the desert, which stretched out to the far horizon.

'How will you know where my old village is?' asked Zuki.

'I got the co-ordinates of where you were picked up by the scouting team who found you. We'll just go north from there – shouldn't be too far out.'

A smudge of green appeared on the horizon, and soon the forest was rolling by beneath them. The transport slowed down, flying over several open glades in the dense tree cover, and then they found it. Nature had already tried to cover up the hideous scar the attackers had wrought on Zuki's village, but a few of the taller stone walls still showed above the new mass of greenery.

'It's a funny feeling,' said Zuki, 'seeing my old village again. I can't believe so much has happened since I left it.'

The transport slowly cruised around, the pilot looking for a suitable place to land. In a clearing between the remains of the village and the animal pens, they could see the big transport which would be their home until a more permanent base was established, and the pilot landed their transport next to it.

'Right,' said Brond, 'once we've got our bits and pieces into our new home, we'll see if we can find the cave where Zuki had his experience. At least it's a starting point.'

They passed what remained of the animal pens, the little stream, and on into the clearing with the rock pile, where Zuki had made his temporary home so long ago.

The stick barrier at the cave entrance had long ago disintegrated, to be replaced with a large green bush which completely covered the hole, and it would have been missed if Zuki hadn't found one or two blackened stones where he had made his fire.

A couple of quick hacks with a blade Brond had fortuitously brought with him, and the cave entrance was exposed.

They had to stoop down to gain entrance, but then the cave expanded out, and they could all stand up. Kono produced a torch, and proceeded to flash it around.

'Is that the hole you crawled into?' asked Kono, pointing to a small dark opening at the back of the cave.

'Yes,' Zuki replied, 'but it was much bigger then. It somehow shrank when I got back into the main cave.'

'That's impossible,' said Kono, 'it's solid rock.'

'I know, and the crystal light thing is impossible too. But it happened, and to you.'

'Well, there's no way we can get in there.' said Brond, 'When the tunnellers come, we'll get them to open it up, and then we can get a sample of the rock the crystal came from. That should give us a clue as to what type of rock to look for. I'll get on to it right away.'

Two hours later the tunnellers arrived and began cutting away the rock. They were unable to use the new laser machine, because it and its power plant were too big, so it was just the drill and explosives.

In the meantime, the five of them walked back past the animal pens, and on to the remains of the village, Zuki explaining how village life had worked. His old cottage was located, and despite Brond's advice not to enter it, he did so, pushing past the new greenery which covered everything.

'I just remembered,' he called back to the others, 'my father saying he had been given a strange box from someone passing through. Neither of them could open it, so he just put in the store where the flour was kept – it might still be there.'

'Be careful,' Brond called out, 'those walls don't look too safe.'

Just behind where Zuki had retrieved the flour container, a blackened something covered in vines lay up against the stone wall. He wriggled it out, and returned to the others, giving it to Brond.

'It's certainly old,' said Brond, 'and covered in a thin layer of metal over something else. I can tell by its weight.'

Despite their efforts, they couldn't open what they thought was the lid, until Brond produced a heavy bladed knife. After a lot of effort, the lid flew open, revealing a pristine interior of shiny metal.

'It seems to be made of wood, or something like it, and covered in a metal sheath, with a metal lining. Looks like I've broken the lock mechanism though.' Brond said.

'Do you think it's the box thing referred to in the old papers?' asked Kono.

'Doubt that,' Brond replied, 'this is just a lined wooden box, but we'll keep just in case.'

By the time they had returned to the cave, the tunnellers had almost broken through to the inner chamber. The passageway between the caves was much shorter than Zuki remembered.

'One more blast, and we're through,' said one of the tunnellers, 'and then it's just a matter of clearing away the rubble and you should be able to get through.'

Although they were stood well outside the cave, the blast made their ears ring, and when the smoke and dust had cleared, they entered the now enlarged tunnel.

'Good God,' exclaimed Zuki, 'there's the remains of the torch I brought in. That proves I was here,' he added.

The torch was flashed all around the cave, and at last they found what they thought was the recess the crystal had lain in, but there was no sign of the crystal. Brond called up to the mineralogist, asking him to make a note of the surrounding rock, and a cast of the crystal's recess – just in case if might provide some useful data.

'I don't think we'll find another crystal here,' said Brond, 'it's just one big rock with smaller ones around it. By taking measurements, we were nearly through to the back of the main block.'

The tunnellers were sent back to base, and then they drew lots as to who would cook up the evening meal.

'Well, that wasn't too bad,' said Brond, after they had eaten, 'although I cooked it myself. But I don't know what we'll get when the fresh stuff runs out, and we have to rely on the concentrates.'

Next day, it was decided to visit one of the tribes who lived along the base of the mountain, to see if there were any tales of the mines in their folklore.

As the transport entered a glade, several men dressed in animal skins and with metal helmets on their heads appeared from the surrounding bushes.

'They look like the lot who burned down our village,' said Zuki quietly.

'Ugly looking sods,' said Kono, fingering the stunner in his pocket.

Brond opened the hatch and stepped out onto the grass.

'We come in peace,' Brond said loudly, 'and mean you no harm.'

This brought two spears swinging their way towards Brond, who neatly stepped aside, and then held up his hand.

'Do not attack us, or you will suffer,' he said firmly.

An arm was raised by one of the men, and the spear point glinted in the sunlight. Brond raised his arm, pointing at the would-be attacker, and he fell to the ground - motionless.

'Drop your weapons now,' he called out authoritatively. As another man raised his spear arm and then dropped to the ground, the other spears were immediately discarded, with a look of fear on the faces of the attackers.

'Where are the mines?' asked Brond, 'Tell me, or you all will be dead.'

After a long pause and a bit of muttering among those still standing…

'What are mines?' came back.

'Mines are holes into the mountain,' Brond said, 'tell me now, or you will all suffer.'

'We have no mines – you come look.'

'He's right, I just sensed that from him,' said Kono, and he stepped forward, one hand in his pocket – and the rest of the attackers fell to the ground in a heap.

'There was no need for that,' said Brond sharply.

'Maybe not,' Kono replied, 'but we won't get any more trouble from them once word gets around. Anyway, once they 'come to', they'll be alright.'

The five of them looked around at the scattered bodies, the geologist commenting that he didn't think they had washed since they were born, Zuki adding he thought the stunning effect probably relaxed their bowls, and they had emptied.

'There's nothing more for us here,' Brond said, 'so let's move on and see what the other groups know.'

They all got back into the transport and headed west, passing through three more settlements. In the first village, as soon as the transport drove into sight, everyone scattered and disappeared, despite Brond yelling out that they 'had come in peace'.

'You won't catch any of that lot,' commented Kono, 'they're too fleet of foot.'

The second little settlement proved to be useless too; they appeared thin and malnourished, with a sullen look, and gave the same answer as the first group to Brond's question, Kono confirming that they weren't lying.

The third clearing looked more promising - a double row of neat stone built single story houses, with roofs made from thin slabs of stone, and smoke coming from several chimneys.

'Well, they at least have fire – looks hopeful.' said Zuki.

As the transport stopped in the middle of the cluster of buildings, a tall man brandishing what looked like a crude rifle came out to meet them.

'Greetings,' called out Brond, the man just nodded his head, and then lowered the gun.

'You don't seem afraid,' said Brond, surprised.

'We seen things like that before,' the man said, pointing at the transport, 'but they usually high up in the sky. Is that one broken?'

'No,' Brond replied, 'this one is meant to travel on the ground only. Can we ask your people some questions about this place?'

'What you want to know?' asked the man.

'We would like to ask a group of your people about some of the old stories from the past,' Brond said, 'that's if you agree to that.'

The man nodded his head again, and went back into his house, returning moments later with what looked like a curved animal horn. Putting it to his mouth, a blast of sound echoed around the houses, making all five of them jump.

'How can such a small thing make such a big noise?' asked Kono, 'I had made a thing like that, but it didn't sound that loud.'

Within minutes, a small neatly dressed crowd had gathered around the transport, staring at the metal monster in their midst, and muttering among themselves. The man with the horn put it to his mouth again, and his voice boomed out across the clearing,

'These people want to ask us about the old legends. They mean us no harm, they just want to talk.'

Brond stepped down from the transport, smiling, and raised his hand in greeting, followed by the other four.

'We are collecting stories from the past,' he said, 'and would like to ask you about your old folk tales.'

Many old tales were recited, and then Brond mentioned the 'holes dug in the mountain' bit, but nothing much was offered.

'Has no one heard about it? Nothing about strange rocks?' he asked again.

An old man bent double, with long white hair stepped forward,

'When I was a boy, some people dressed like you came here, and showed us some rocks. They wanted to know if we had any, and where they were. We had not seen the rocks before, and told them. They got cross and went away.'

Brond thanked him for his tale, and the others for theirs, waved goodbye, and got aboard the transport.

'Now that's interesting,' said Brond, 'looks like someone has been nosing around for the crystals. Or maybe it was just a mineralogist looking for a specific ore. I think we're getting closer to our goal, though,' he added.

After a couple of hours, and no sign of another village, they came to a deep rift in the landscape. It looked as if the ground had split and moved apart revealing a deep ravine of some hundred metres. They stopped the transport, got out, and went over to the edge.

'My God,' exclaimed Zuki, 'that's one hell of a drop, and it looks as if there's water at the bottom.'

'If you look closely,' said Brond, 'you'll see a water mark about halfway up. But to fill it up to that mark would take an awful lot of water. So where does it all go? It's solid rock, right to the bottom.'

'More to the point,' said geologist, 'where does it come from? Normal rainfall wouldn't account for that amount.'

'I think we should photograph this.' Kono said, and ran back to the transport to get a camera.

'Looks like a sort of big hole down there,' he said, pointing, 'right near the bottom.'

'The only thing I can think of,' said the geologist, 'is that there must be a massive lake up on the mountain somewhere, and a passageway from the bottom of the lake which sweeps up and then down to the bottom of this rift. When the mountain lake reaches a certain level, you would get a siphon effect, and the lake would drain, filling this rift to the water mark – and then the whole thing would start all over again as the mountain lake fills up.'

'Should be quite a show when it takes place then,' commented Zuki.

'But where does it all go?' asked Kono, not at all sure of the whole set up, 'It's nearly empty now.'

Before anyone could answer, a deep rumbling could be heard, and a faint trembling of the ground beneath their feet could just be felt.

'Everybody back,' Brond called out, 'something is about to happen.' But Zuki stayed at the edge of the precipice.

'Hey, come and look at this,' he called out, 'a trickle of water is coming out of that hole.'

They all edged forward again, cautiously – and then there was a united gasp.

The trickle had increased to a reasonable flow, and then with a roar which echoed around the rift as the siphon got down to the serious business of emptying the lake above. The force of the water was so strong, that it flew out of the hole horizontally for about a hundred metres before curving down to the rift bottom.

'If I hadn't seen that, I wouldn't have believed it,' Brond said, 'and look how quickly it's filling the rift.'

The roar diminished as the water rose above the hole from which it was emitting, and the five of them stood there, transfixed at the spectacle of nature at its most powerful.

Twenty minutes later, and the water had reached the water mark on the side of the rift, and they stood waiting to see what would happen next.

Suddenly, the water level began to drop, and they all leaned forward to see where it was going. But there was no clue as to where it went, as the level continued to drop at the same rate it had filled the rift.

Twenty minutes later, and the bare rock of the rift's bottom was exposed, and they were just in time to see a huge slab of square rock slam into place at the opposite end of the rifts base, and felt a faint shudder beneath their feet.

'That will take a bit of explaining,' Brond said to the geologist, 'and you can't tell me that was a work of nature.'

'I would agree with you on that,' came the reply, 'that system has been constructed, but to what purpose?'

'You may well ask,' Brond replied, 'I doubt we'll ever find out – not much is known about this region.'

They all climbed back into the transport and had to go south to go around the end of the rift, and then it was back on course.

Because of the roughness of the new terrain, it took almost an hour to reach the next sign of a clearing. Tilled fields heralded something a little different, and then they came to the dwellings – well constructed two story houses, with a wide road between them.

'This looks more like civilisation,' said Kono, 'they've even got some sort of a town square.'

Chapter 10
First contact

THE TRANSPORT SLOWED down, and then stopped in the middle of the square. What few people that were about just stopped and stared at the huge machine. A few moments later a uniformed figure appeared, and purposely strode up to the transport. Brond had already opened the hatch and was about to step down to the ground.

'Welcome, I am the community's representative.' the man said, 'Why have you come here? We know of the so called 'masters'. I assume you are one of them?'

'We are not 'masters' of anything,' Brond said calmly, 'we are part of the same race, it's just that you have chosen to live out here, and forgo all scientific advancements, and we have chosen to use them to our advantage.'

'What is your purpose of coming here then?' the man enquired.

Brond thought the 'story telling' excuse wouldn't cut much ice, so he tried something else.

'We are searching for a certain type of mineral, as a small quantity is needed for our research. Would you be willing to help us, please?'

'I will have to consult the other councillors first, but I would think that would be possible.'

And with that, he returned to the house he had come out of.

'Well, this lot seem friendly and co-operative,' Brond commented, 'but I haven't figured out how to question them yet.'

'Just show them the samples we took from my cave,' said Zuki, 'and see if they know where there might be more of it.'

'Thanks Zuki, yes, keep it simple and straight forward.' And he went to the cooking area, it was his turn to prepare the evening meal, and the light was beginning to fail.

No approach was made by the 'chief' that night, but next morning several members of the tribe were waiting outside the transport when Brond opened the hatch to go out.

'Good morning gentlemen-' began Brond.

'We are not gentle men,' said the chief representative, 'we are members of the council. We understand you are looking for a certain mineral, and we are willing to help you, if you can give us details of what you require.'

'I'll just get it,' said Brond, 'and thank you for your co-operation.'

One by one, the council members scrutinised the sample, and in turn shook their heads.

'It would seem that none of us recognise this material.' said the chief, 'What makes you think it could be found here?'

'We know it can be found somewhere along the foot of this mountain,' said Brond, 'we just don't know where, and your village was the next place on our list. Some villages have stories of making holes into the mountain – I suppose it could have come from such work.'

'Leave the sample with us, and we will show it to all our people. Someone might know where it can be found, but I've never heard of making holes in the mountain.' said the chief.

Brond gave the man a small piece of the rock, thanked him profusely, and re-entered the transport.

Next morning, the chief was waiting outside the transport.

'We are sorry, but no one has seen this type of stone. But there was one old man who thought he may have a story from the past to interest you. Would you like to see him?'

'Yes please,' said Brond, 'any stories or legends may contain a clue which we can follow up.'

Later than morning, the chief plus a couple of the other councillors helped an old man, almost bent double and with long white hair, up to the transport where the five explorers were waiting. Zuki immediately went back into the transport, unclipped a chair from its clamp, and bade the old man to sit down.

'So, you have some old tales to tell.' Brond began, 'We would be very interested to hear yours – if you would like to tell us.'

'It is only an old story my father used to tell me when I was a child,' the old man croaked, 'he said his grandfather had told him, when he was a boy.'

'That sounds interesting,' Brond said in an encouraging voice, 'carry on.'

'There was one story about the masters coming to his village, and giving nice gifts to anyone would help them. But when they went with the masters, we never saw them again, and so we distrusted the masters, and would have nothing to do with them. He used to say his father said he would send him to the masters if he misbehaved.'

The old man began to cough, so Zuki went into the transport to get him a drink.

'There was another tale my father told me about strange lights in the mountain, which no one must look at. If they did, awful things would happen to them – that's why we didn't go playing about on the mountain.' The old man rubbed his throat gently, and more drink was offered.

'This is very good,' the old man said, 'do you want another tale?'

Zuki nodded his head.

'Watch it,' Kono quietly said to Brond in an aside, 'that old boy likes the drink, and he thinks he's onto a good thing with these stories. He's trying to find something more to say – he'll possibly make it up.'

'When I was a boy, we used to go up onto the mountain looking for the lights, but we didn't find any. Some people said they had seen them in the distance, but when they approached them, they moved away.'

'Yep,' said Kono in a hushed voice. Brond nodded, and said quietly,

'Fetch the old boy a bottle of fruit concentrate and show him how to dilute it. He deserves something for his trouble.'

'Thank you all very much for your help,' Zuki said, 'we'll add these stories to those we've collected earlier. But now we must continue our search for the strange stone.'

The councillors helped the old man away, and the crew readied the transport for the next stage of their exploration. They left the little township, turned north, and headed for the foot of the mountain range.

'I think that last story was a bit suspect,' said Zuki, 'but the others somehow rang true – but it's all we've got so far. It all happened a long time ago, so I suppose any spoil tips or workings will be covered in vegetation by now.'

The ground they were travelling on began to rise, and the mountain loomed ahead, dark and menacing, huge boulders having fallen in the past were blocking their way and the transport had to work its way between them.

'We'll head east with respect to the village,' said Brond, 'and then west along the foot of the mountain. That should cover the main area most likely to have been used – look out for any flat areas or mounds that don't look as if they should be there.'

Crawling along the base of the mountain, and an hour later, the first sign of something unusual appeared.

'That flat area ahead doesn't really fit in with the general landscape,' said Zuki, 'I'd like to stop here and dig down a bit.'

After they had removed about two hundred centimetres of grass and soil, they came to a layer of crushed stone. After repeating the process a few metres further on, and again hitting stone, they were convinced that man had been at work here – but a long time ago.

'There's no sign of any old buildings,' Brond said, 'and I would have expected something to remain – dwellings or storage sheds.'

'Maybe they used portable ones,' Zuki replied, 'you'd get quite a few on this flattened area. Someone's put a lot of work in here, so it must have been quite important.' He added.

'And that ridge up there,' said the geologist, pointing to an area several hundred metres up the slope, 'looks a bit too flat to be natural. It might be worth a look at.'

'Right,' said Brond, 'let's take a break for lunch, and then we'll take a hike up there.'

When they reached the top of the ridge, they were in for two surprises.

'This area is huge,' said Zuki, 'it didn't show how wide it is from down below, and it looks as if there's a track leading down from it at the far end. A vast amount of material must have been dug out of somewhere to make this.'

'And look over there,' Brond said, 'that huge boulder must have rolled down from above, but next to it is a dark area. Could be a hole.'

The five ran over to the boulder, and as they went around the side of it, the opening into the mountain became apparent.

'My God, that's one big hole,' exclaimed Kono, 'we could get our rock blaster in there with room to spare.'

'I'll send for it if we can go in far enough, and it looks as if we are on the right track for those crystals – that's if they exist here. So, it's back to the transport for torches, and anything else you think we may need.'

When they were fully kitted up, including a good supply of food and water, they approached the dark and sombre hole in the side of the mountain.

'Well, this has defiantly been cut by man, or something.' Brond announced, 'You can see the cut marks of tools. Wonder why they made it so big? Not really necessary for normal mining operations, I would have thought.'

Soon they were in a deep blackness, except for the beams of their torches, and looking back, the entrance was just a tiny pinpoint of light in the far distance behind them.

'Look out for holes where crystals might have been,' Zuki called out, his voice echoing down the long tunnel, 'one of you should have the cast we made from my cave to give you an idea of what it looks like.'

'I've got it,' the geologist answered, 'not seen anything yet.'

'The air in here is very dry,' said Brond, 'better stop for a drink,' which they did, and then continued on into the blackness ahead

The floor of the tunnel began to slope upwards, when an excited cry from the geologist halted them in their tracks.

'Look,' he said, 'I've found a hole, and the cast fits perfectly.'

'Well, I'll be damned,' said the mineralogist, 'so they really existed.'

And they all gathered round, each fitting the cast into the recess, just to be sure it was real.

'I wonder how they knew where to start the tunnel?' asked Kono, 'I doubt they'd have just dug in at random.'

'From what I understand,' said Zuki, 'it was just someone digging for some mineral or other that came across the first one, got 'changed', and it all took off from there. So, they just enlarged the tunnel from the old workings. But why they made it so big, I don't know.'

The trudged on for another hour and were feeling the strain of walking so long in such an alien environment, when another crystal recess was found.

'That's only two holes we've found.' said Kono, 'I wonder what made them persist, bearing in mind the hard work involved.'

'I know we've only found two holes,' said Brond, 'but we may well have missed some. Up on the roof of the tunnel, for instance; we'll go on for another ten minutes, and then return to the transport. I think we've done enough for the first day.'

They were just about to turn back, when the end of the tunnel came in sight, just a blank wall of rock confronted them.

'So that's the end of it,' said Kono, sounding disappointed, 'bit of a let down.'

'Come on Kono,' said Brond, 'we've as near as damn proved the crystals existed here. So there's a good chance there'll be more – it's just a matter of finding them.'

The journey back to the transport seemed to drag on for ages, and then they saw the little pinpoint of light up ahead, and they were soon out in the open.

'Never thought fresh air could taste so good.' Zuki said, breathing in deeply, 'Although it was exciting, I can't say I'd do it for a pastime.'

Brond called up the mine cutting machine and set up a radio beacon for them to home onto, announcing it would take a couple of days to reach them.

After a good meal, they all slept soundly that night, but next morning were at a loose end as to what to do. No one thought it a good idea to return to the tunnel, as there was little to do there except look for more crystal holes. But that was non-productive, as the first two proved the point for the expedition.

'I think we should explore the whole site,' said Brond, 'there may be some more clues as to exactly who was at work here – and we may have missed something important.'

They walked the whole length of the ridge plateau and found several large blocks of what looked like concrete, where machines of some sort may have been mounted, but there was no clue as to what they might have been.

The mineralogist had climbed up some way on the rock face, and was busily hacking away at the surface, when Brond asked him what he was doing it for.

'The rock is a little different here, so I though I'd see what's beneath it – if anything.'

A large slab of rock came free, nearly taking the mineralogist with it, and crashed to the ground, narrowly missing Brond.

'My God, I've found one,' the man called out.

'Don't look at it,' Brond yelled back, 'cover it with anything, your shirt or any lose stones, but don't look at it! And get down here quickly.'

The man almost fell the last few metres, winding up in a heap at Brond's feet.

'What was it like?' asked Brond.

'Sort of like smoky glass, with a bright light inside it. I felt the urge to get closer, but did what you said. Do you think it's affected me?' he asked worriedly.

'No, I don't think so,' Brond replied, 'you weren't up there long enough, and you didn't pass out, so you should be OK.'

The team gathered up several flat pieces of rock, and passed them up to Brond, who was just below where the crystal was found; when he had what he thought were enough pieces, climbed up the last metre or so, and covered the crystal up, returning to the ground, shaking.

'What do we do with it now?' asked the man.

'We leave it where it is, until we can figure out how to make one of those special boxes, and God knows how we do that.'

'Maybe that old burnt box I found in my home is what they put the crystals in after all,' said Zuki, 'you only need to keep the light from them, I think.'

'OK, we'll get some of them made,' Brond replied, 'only hope they work. Draw up some plans, and I'll get it done. Oh, and we'll send them the original one. Just thought, how do we pick the damned things up?' Zuki just shrugged his shoulders in reply.

The tunnelling machine arrived early in the morning, and using the newly found track at the end of the ridge, was manoeuvred into position, ready for the next phase of the crystal hunt. A small self-powered truck came with it for the removal of the debris, and once it was known that the gear was on site, breakfast was speedily consumed.

All five of them scrambled up the slope to the ridge plateau, trying to be first to reach the tunneller. But it had come with its own driver, who politely explained it needed an experienced operator to use it safely.

The machine was a little different to the one Zuki had seen, and had been improved. This one had a pair of hydraulically operated arms to scoop the debris onto a conveyer, which then loaded onto the truck.

All they could do was watch as the machine trundled up the tunnel, aligned itself with the blank tunnel end, and went into action.

They had somehow filtered out the white light component of the laser, so the work face could be seen, just about, as it crumbled in small fragments, and was swept away into the disposal truck.

After fifteen truck loads had been sent down to the outside plateau, the end wall collapsed in a shower of dust and small stones, and they were through to the large cavity beyond. The mining machine was withdrawn, the debris cleared, and the five eagerly moved forward to see what lay beyond the opening.

They stood there, dumbfounded at what they saw. The tunneller had broken through to another tunnel, but this one was different. They had broken though at a curved section, and the tunnel was a little larger than the one they had made, its walls and floor were as smooth as glass, and with no tool marks showing.

Chapter 11
The Ancients

'WHAT THE HELL have we found?' asked Brond, but no one answered, they had no answers.

'This wasn't made by our race.' Zuki said, 'We couldn't have done it, even with our new machine – and nothing existed like our machine that long ago.'

The new tunnel walls seem to glow with an inner light, so the torches were switched off while they decided what to do next.

'We could just walk on, and see where it leads.' said Kono, 'But we'd better draw a map as we go along, in case there are any junctions and we get lost.'

They had walked for nearly half an hour along the featureless tunnel, and were about to turn back, when it opened out into an enormous hall. The floor was covered in a pattern of metal studs in small groups, while the wall nearest to them also had studs protruding from its surface.

No one said anything for a while, and the Brond spoke in a hushed voice,

'This reminds me of a machine shop, where all the machines have been removed, and the mounting studs have been left behind. But it's so big – what the hell were they making?'

'I know this sounds improbable,' said Zuki, 'but I think this is alien. We couldn't have done it. Look, there's an opening over there, lets see where that leads.'

'Got this on your map, Kono?' asked Brond.

'Yes,' he answered, 'and I've marked the point where we came in.'

The studs which protruded from the floor were not quite as random as they had first thought, there being a clear path between groups, and soon they were at the opening in the far wall. They had only gone a short distance when they came to the first room.

'It hasn't got a door,' said Kono, 'that's a bit odd, isn't it? And look there's a sort of bunk bed thing.'

'Yes, and it's built into the wall. Perhaps that's why it wasn't taken away with all the other stuff,' said the geologist.

As they went along the passage, they counted forty or so rooms on each side of the passage, and then gave up counting.

The passage finally came to an end, but the floor has a square section on, and no one went any further. Brond looked upwards, and announced that the square shape was also on the ceiling.

'That looks like a lift compartment,' he said, 'and I'm not going to stand on it!'

'Should be safe,' Zuki said, 'I doubt there's any power on – but you never know.'

Just then they could hear a faint distant roaring noise, and they turned to look at each other.

'Come on, say what you all are thinking,' said Zuki, 'it's that water thing, in the ravine.'

The others nodded.

Kono kept a faithful map of their progress, and many more rooms were discovered – all having been emptied of everything which wasn't actually built into the walls or floor.

'Pity there no pictures on the walls,' said Brond, 'it would give us an idea of what they looked like. I still find it hard to believe that an alien race lived here, it's just too preposterous. But then we're actually in it, by the looks of things.'

'They must have left something behind,' said Zuki, 'no one is that tidy – it's just a matter of finding it.'

The search paid off in the end. Kono had been trailing behind, when he noticed a small unlit passage branching off the main one.

'Hold on,' he called out, 'I think I've found something. This side passage isn't giving out any light, and it looks as if there is something in there.'

The others hurried back to see what he had found and flashed their torches around to reveal a machine of some kind.

'I think it's some type of transport.' said Zuki, 'It's got what looks like six seats in pairs, and one for the driver in the front, and look, there's a sort of control panel.'

'It can't be a transport,' said Brond, 'it hasn't got any wheels – it's flat on the ground.'

Before anyone could stop him, Zuki had climbed into the driver's seat.

'For God's sake, don't twiddle anything,' Brond called out, 'we don't know what does.'

'We should be so lucky, I doubt it'll do anything after all this time,' Zuki responded, 'but I could just try this one.' His finger hovered over a button, and at that precise moment Brond's hand slipped, and pushed Zuki's arm.

There was faint hum, and the machine rose off the ground about ten centre metres, swayed slightly, and went down again with a loud thump.

There was complete silence, apart from the echoes of the thump, dying away in the distance.

'So, it is a transport,' Zuki said, 'and it hovers above the ground. That should be a new bit of tech for our researchers to get their teeth into, we don't have anything like that. Whatever power it had must have drained away over time, with just a tiny bit left.'

'Just as well,' muttered Brond quietly.

The geologist was flashing his torch around the walls, when he said,

'These walls are slightly damp, perhaps that interferes with whatever makes the walls give out light – the other walls are bone dry. Maybe they missed this machine in the dark when they took everything else away.'

'Mark it on your map,' Brond said.

'Already done it,' Kono replied.

They carried on down the passage, looking into any rooms in the sidewalls, but they were all empty. And then they came to the shaft. Luckily, there was a metal barrier across the passage, or they could have fallen down it.

'My God,' exclaimed Brond, flashing his torch around 'it's absolutely huge.'

The shaft must have been fifty metres across, and went down to the inky depths below, also rising well above their heads.

'What the hell is that all about?' asked Brond, leaning over the rails, 'Turn your beams onto long distance, let's see just how far down it goes.'

Five tight beams of light lanced down into the still blackness below, and still they didn't reach the bottom.

'OK, let's look up.'

They swung their torches up, but there was no end to the shaft that they could see.

'It must have a purpose,' Brond said, 'and it must have taken a long time and a great deal of labour to hack that lot out – and where did they put it?'

'Pity we don't have anything we could throw down to gauge its depth,' said Zuki, 'but they've left nothing laying around. Tidy lot.'

'We'll carry on looking for anything left for a few more minutes,' Brond ordered, 'and then we'd better head back – we've come a long way. There's a turning off back there, we'll take that.'

They marched on, checking every break in the tunnel walls for rooms, but they were all empty – until they came to a break in the glass smooth walls. Beyond which was a space, more like a cave than a room cut from the solid rock.

'Well, this is different,' said Zuki, 'looks like some old mining tools over there, and there's a block of something.'

'This looks like a natural formation,' said the geologist, 'formed by a large bubble of gas when this lot was molten – there are no tool marks that I can see.'

Kono had gone over to the block-like object, kicked it to make sure it was inactive, and then picked it up.

'Hey, Zuki,' he called out, 'it looks like one of your box things, take a look.'

'You're right,' Zuki replied, after examining it, 'its lined with metal and so is the outside. But the box itself isn't wood, look here where some of the metal has peeled back, it's like a foamed plastic. Otherwise, in principle, it's the same sort of thing.'

Brond had gone over to the far corner of the cave, and was kicking the lose stones and bits of rock which had fallen over the ages to one side, so that he didn't miss anything.

'You'd better come and have a look at this,' he said, excitement in his voice.

They crowded around Brond, who was blowing the dust of ages off what appeared to be a book.

'It can't be made of paper,' said Zuki, 'or it would have disintegrated by now. So what's it made of?'

'Looks like some sort of metal, but none I've ever seen,' Brond replied, 'it's quite flexible and soft, but tough.'

The first few pages were covered in some kind of strange script, and then they came to the picture. It showed a man-like creature, much like themselves, but dressed differently, holding a gleaming piece of rock.

'He doesn't look too different to us,' said the mineralogist.

'But not as ugly as the aliens.' Kono added, 'Seems a bit odd though, we now have three races, all looking similar.'

'Not odd really,' said Zuki, 'if you think about it, the human form is probably the best adapted for making and doing things and getting around. I wouldn't be surprised if all sentient life developed this way, wherever it began.'

They thumbed through the remaining pages, but they were covered in script, except for the last page, which had a picture.

'It's a star chart,' said Brond, 'and that's our system.' pointing to it, 'That mark there is possibly where they've gone - but how?'

'We don't know what they were making,' Zuki said, 'maybe it was a spaceship.'

'But why leave this planet?' asked the geologist.

'Let's face it,' Brond responded, 'this world doesn't have a lot going for it. We have the temperate band going around the equator where we live, but the rest is mainly desert. We'll take the box and this book thing back with us. Maybe the language lab can decipher it.'

They checked the cave for anything else left behind, but there was nothing. So referring to Kono's map, they began the long journey back to the outside world.

After a good meal, they sat back and tried to relax, but the excitement of their finds in the underground complex had not died down - if anything, it was still growing. Many were the theories put forward as to what had happened to the people in the mountain, and what the strange box thing might have been used for. Crystal capture, strangely, was not among them. It was only later, when the picture of the man holding the glowing stone was looked at closely, that Zuki thought it might be a crystal still mainly embedded in the piece of rock.

And then Brond put forward the theory that the people of the mountain had found the crystals, advanced themselves to a point where they had developed space travel, and left.

They were about to call it a day, when Kono suddenly said,

'I know this might sound a bit odd, but I have just had the feeling that the cave we found could be where some crystals might be found.'

'What makes you think that?' asked Brond, still a little sceptical about finding crystals, 'We didn't find anything there, except bits of fallen rock, the box, and the book.'

'I know it's a bit of a long shot, but we know where one crystal is. Outside, where we covered it up with stones. I just wondered if we brought it into the cave, put out the lights, the crystal might try and communicate, or whatever it does, with any remaining crystals there.'

'Funny you should say that, Kono,' Zuki added, 'I've been thinking along similar lines. It's worth a try, we don't have anything else to go by.'

'There's one thing we haven't resolved,' said Brond, 'and that's how do we pick them up? I don't feel like just grabbing them in my hand, that's if we find any.'

'We could use tongs,' Zuki offered, 'I remember being drawn towards the crystal, so it only works if you are close enough; the person with the tongs would have their eyes covered, and be guided by someone else a little distance away, who wouldn't be affected.'

'Hmm...' Brond didn't sound too convinced.

Next morning, Brond made an announcement, as they ate their first meal of the day,

'Right, let's give it a try. It seems to be the only option we have at the moment. Firstly, I'll send the mineralogist and the geologist back to base. I have already made security arrangements for their silence about what we are doing, and all other personnel can leave also – they don't know about the crystals at all. That just leaves us three here. If we do find any, it must be kept to us three. No one else must have an inkling about the crystals – and I mean no one.'

'But they will be used?' queried Zuki.

'Yes,' Brond replied, 'but very carefully, and only when really needed. They are too precious to be used at random, just because someone feels like it.'

The holding boxes Brond ordered had arrived, along with a small self powered truck, and Kono had made a crude pair of tongs.

'Once everyone has left the site,' said Brond, 'load the boxes into the truck along with anything else you think we might need, and we'll go for the crystal the mineralogist found near the tunnel entrance, and then we go for the cave.'

It was late morning before they were alone, and then the truck was packed with boxes and an assortment of tools. Zuki volunteered to retrieve the crystal they had covered up by the tunnel entrance, wrapping a piece of cloth around his eyes as he got ready to remove the stones from the crystal. Kono had climbed up a short distance away, but in full view of their target, and called out instructions to Zuki.

'Hey, I can see it now,' Kono called out, 'the tongs are just above it. A bit to your right, and lower the tongs about twenty centimeters. OK, close 'em. You've got it!' he called out, his voice rising with excitement.

'Move to your left, a bit more. You're over the box, lower about ten centimeters and release. Now close the lid.'

Zuki removed the cloth from his eyes and scrambled down to ground level.

'Well, that's one, now for the rest.' He said.

They entered the tunnel with Zuki in the driving seat, and he suggested the other two sit on the boxes, to save the long walk to the cave.

The truck's lights lit the tunnel up far better than their torches had done, and several more holes where crystals had been were located.

'That's twenty-three I've counted so far,' said Kono, 'and I bet I've missed some. No wonder they advanced so much, their intelligence must have gone through the roof.'

'I've been trying to work out how the crystal thing works,' Zuki called back from his seat, 'I think it only works on what you've got already. It sort of restores your memory of everything you've learnt, and sharpens up your thinking ability. That's how it worked for me.'

'Not much hope for Brond, then,' Kono leaned forward, whispering with a chuckle in Zuki's ear.

'Wouldn't be too sure of that,' Zuki replied, 'he's a lot brighter than I first thought.'

They reached the cave without mishap but had to be careful while manoeuvring around the studded floor of the huge machine shop, still marvelling at the enormity of it.

'Right,' said Zuki, 'you both stand behind me. I'll cover my eyes, just in case, and I'll then open the box, tilting it towards the cave wall. Look out for any hint of extra light spots on the walls. I think they somehow link up with each other. Right – lights out. Let your eyes get used to the darkness.'

The blackness was almost palpable, and Brond gave a little cough, just to reassure himself that he still existed.

'Hey, I can feel something,' said Kono, 'it's like the cave is closing in on us.'

'I'm opening the lid now,' said Zuki.

The light from the crystal lit the cave up dimly, and then it began to pulse very slightly.

'I can see two other bright spots on the wall,' said Brond, 'shall I mark them?'

'Yes,' replied Zuki, 'but don't look back this way or you'll see my crystal.'

It took nearly half an hour to mark all the positions of light spots on the wall of the cave, stopping when the boxed crystal stopped pulsing.

'I can't help thinking there's some form of intelligence here,' said Zuki, after closing the lid on the box, 'it's almost as if the crystal was trying to help us mark the others.'

'Come on,' Brond replied, 'it's only a mineral. Albeit a bit special, I'll admit.'

Kono turned the lights of the truck back on, and the cave was flooded in light, the marks Brond had put on the walls showing up clearly.

'Now what?' asked Brond.

'Same procedure as before.' Zuki replied, 'One of you chip away the rock over the mark until the crystal is exposed, but don't look at it. I'll hold the box and tongs, and someone guide me to grasp it and get it into the box.'

By the time they had collected all the crystals, they were utterly exhausted, and flopped down on the cave floor.

'Well, we've done it,' said Kono, 'but I wouldn't like to do this too often.'

Food and drink were passed around, and then Brond began to snore, until he got a dig in the ribs from Kono.

'How many crystals have we got?' asked Kono.

'Thirty-one,' Zuki replied, 'including the one from outside. You know, that odd feeling we got when we first came into this cave has gone. At least, I can't feel it any more.'

'Do you really think the crystals wanted to be found?' asked Brond, 'I can't really get my head around that.'

'Yes, I do,' said Zuki, 'I can't really explain it, but that's the feeling I got when I found the first crystal as a boy. There are some things in nature, for want of a better word, that we can't explain, and maybe never will. But that doesn't mean they don't exist.'

'One thing I'd like to do before we leave here,' said Brond, 'is to take some of these rocks and drop 'em down that shaft.'

They collected up some of the biggest rocks, made their way to the railings guarding the shaft, and dropped the first one down. With their torches on tight beam, they were able to see the rock drop into the depths beneath until it dwindled out of sight, but there was no noise of it hitting the bottom.

'God, that thing's deep,' muttered Brond, 'I wish we knew what it's for.'

'Could be a giant lift shaft,' said Kono, 'it's unnecessarily big for a ventilation shaft.'

'And it's dark at the top,' said Bono, 'surely there should be light at the top if it was open to the sky.'

'Not necessarily so,' Zuki said, 'if it's long enough all you'd see is the same as the night sky, just darkness. Hey, wait a minute, put the lights out and let our eyes get used to the dark.'

All the torches were switched off, and the blackness rushed in.

'Well, I'll be damned,' exclaimed Brond, 'you're right, I can see some stars. Not many, but some. So it is open to the sky – why didn't we see that before when we looked up?'

'Probably because we had the torches on,' Zuki replied, 'and our eyes were used to that light level. So, it probably is a lift shaft, and they may have got their space ship out that way.'

They returned to the cave, the mystery of the shaft sort of solved, but not completely.

The pile of boxed crystals was loaded onto the truck. Zuki got into the driving seat and they were on their way back to the outside world.

They all slept well that night, some mysteries solved, and their mission almost accomplished.

'Right,' said Brond next morning, 'we'll tidy up the site, and leave the truck a little way inside the tunnel – well out of sight. There's just a slim chance we may have to return, but I doubt it.'

'What will we do with the crystals?' asked Kono.

'They will be locked away safely, and only used when really necessary.' Brond said, 'These are not playthings; we are very fortunate to have knowledge of them, and to have actually found some.'

The journey back to the complex took four days in the land-based transport, and the group were glad to get back to familiar surroundings.

There were only three of the carrier aliens left, and no one could figure out why so many had died. The lone alien was still in good health, and when they visited it, was keen to engage in conversation through the translating equipment.

For the first time, it seemed to regret the aggression it had shown in the beginning, and was more than co-operative to their questions, although they didn't learn much more.

Brond had the crystal boxes stored away in the dungeon-like cells below the complex, with the highest security possible. Only he, Zuki and Kono had access – and two of the three had to agree to that.

One day, Brond got them both together to put an idea to them he'd been mulling over.

'I have been studying the Chief Councillor, and in my estimation, he is a little different to most of us. I think it might be a good idea for him to experience a crystal. So far, he has made all the right decisions in just about everything he's had a hand in, and I wondered if an enhanced CC might be a good thing for us all, and our world. What do you two think?'

'Sounds a good idea,' said Zuki, 'I have no objections, that's if he's up for it.'

'I agree, also,' Kono added, 'three of us with added abilities should make a strong team in times of need.'

'What about you, Brond?' asked Zuki, 'Surely you'd like to have increased abilities?'

'I've thought about it,' he replied, 'but I think I'll stay as I am, for the time being.'

Chapter 12
The Secret's out

Some time later, Brond approached the Chief Councillor and explained to him what their secret mission had been all about.

'I have heard of such things' he said, 'but it seemed so unbelievable that I gave it little credence. You mean you have actually found some?'

'Yes,' Brond replied, 'and two of my associates have actually experienced them. Quite by accident in one case – that's how I came to discover the whole thing. You may know of Zuki, he was the first, and he has proved his worth in handling the alien situation, as you may well know.'

'Yes, I've heard he has been of great benefit to us all with regard to the alien situation. I trust he has been suitably rewarded for his work.'

'So far, we haven't figured out how to reward him. Not that he seeks reward, but it would seem fair if we could. The main point of this meeting is to ask you if you would be willing to experience a crystal enhancement.'

The Chief Councillor looked stunned for a moment, before replying,

'Before I decide, I would like to meet this Zuki, and see just what is involved. Can you arrange it for me?'

'Yes, certainly,' Brond replied, 'I'm sure he would be only too pleased to do so.'

The following day, Zuki found himself in the highly exalted corridors of the main building for Planetary Affairs. A smartly uniformed guide ushered him along with utmost courtesy, and soon they were outside the huge bronze doors of the Chief Councillor's room. The guide indicated he should stand before the doors, while he took three smart steps back, and waited.

'Please come in,' a firm but friendly sounding voice said, and the doors swung open. To say the room was opulent would be an understatement, and Zuki was somewhat surprised. A magnificent dark wooden desk sat before a huge crystal glass window, overlooking the park area beneath. Behind the desk, and rising to his feet, a tall man of middle years smiled at Zuki, and held out his hand.

Zuki was still looking around the room, trying to take it all in when his gaze returned to the man behind the desk, and he stepped forward to touch hands.

'A plain room with a desk and chair is all that's really needed, but

I inherited this from my predecessor.' said the man, still smiling, 'Please, take a seat. I understand you are Zuki – of alien battle fame. I would personally like to thank you for what you have done for us all.'

For the first time in his life, Zuki was stuck for the right words.

'I have asked you here,' said the man, 'to tell me what you know about these crystals, and the affect they can have when exposed to them. I understand you have had your own experience of them. Would you please relate your story?'

Zuki began with the attack on his village, finding the first crystal and what happened, his visit to Kono's world and how it affected him, the battle with the aliens, and the finding of the hoard of crystals in the Outlands.

'How has it affected you, compared to how you were before?' asked the man, 'That is what I'm interested in.'

Zuki explained how he was able to assess things at lightening speed, amass huge amounts of data with ease, and to some extent, be able to see the outcome of multiple situations when under pressure.

'Can you explain how the crystals do this?' asked the man.

'Not really, all I know is that I felt drawn to the crystal as soon as the light got bright, and then I felt compelled to touch it. At that point, I passed out. When I came to, I felt strangely alive, and as time passed, I was able to do things I couldn't do before. It's only my theory, but I think the crystals have some sort of life force in them, and it wants to get out. Whether it is still in me, I don't know, but I don't think so. I think it has boosted my abilities as a 'thank you' maybe – but that is only conjecture. The odd thing is, after the event, there was only a hole where the crystal had been – so where did it go? Anyway, I think it's a benign thing, and certainly wishes us no harm.'

'Thank you for explaining.' said the man, 'It is certainly tempting to have one's abilities lifted up a little. I will consider this over the next few days, and let Brond know.'

Zuki felt somehow the conversation had been terminated, felt he ought to bow, but didn't, and left the room. The man who had guided him there was waiting, smiled, and indicated the way out.

Brond was waiting for him as he left the building, and together they walked over to the transport, and climbed aboard.

'How did it go?' asked Brond, 'He seems a nice almost ordinary sort of fellow, but that's only what you see on the surface. Believe you me, he's as shrewd as they come, and I think a great candidate for enhancement.'

'Well, I thought he was a very nice person, and put me at ease.' Zuki replied, 'But as you say, there is something else there, but well covered up,'

'Oh, and another bit of news,' said Brond, 'the last of the carrier aliens has died – and no one knows why, despite a post-mortem. The one from the attack force is still doing well and has really made himself at home.'

'He would.' Zuki said. As they entered the complex, a man ran up to them and handed Brond note.

'Good God, you'd better read this,' said Brond, handing it to Zuki, 'it's from the language people.'

The note explained that the writing in the strange book they had received for translation bore some similarities to the words on the crashed alien ship's instruments.

For a moment, Zuki just seemed to freeze, and then he said,

'It a long shot, but I would like to take the book to our alien, and watch his reaction when he sees it.'

'That's OK with me.' Brond said, 'The language team can't seem to get any further with it. There are only a few similar words, not enough to make translation possible.'

Zuki retrieved the copy of the strange book from the language department and went to visit the only remaining alien. He was never sure if it was pleased to see him, or anyone else for that matter, as no emotion showed on its face. Over the last few visits, it had been very co-operative when questioned, which was a change from their first encounter with it.

The translation equipment had been improved and rebuilt, and the translation codes extended considerably. It was now possible to hold a reasonable conversation with the alien, although a few words were still missing. Maybe it didn't have an equivalent for them, Kono thought.

Although the alien was humanoid, there were differences to Zuki's people, and the others from the complex. Its skin was a dirty brown/grey colour, and looked hard and dry, but on the odd occasion when their hands had touched, it seemed soft enough. The facial features were hard and set, no emotion showing whatever happened, and the hair on its head was more like the bristles on a scrubbing brush, and were always the same length, and didn't look as if they were ever cut. Zuki wondered how its creators had achieved such genetic changes to their race, and why.

The alien and Zuki sat down opposite each other across the table and exchanged their usual greetings.

'You tell us about your people?' asked Zuki.

'Yes – what?' came back.

'You all one race?' There was along pause.

'Yes – some different.'

'Tell me.' said Zuki. Another long pause, as if the alien was trying to find the right words.

'Leader people, clever, not many. Me people, very few, no fear, we look for things. Many, many other people, do work, make things, simple, not like me.'

'Have your people always been like this?' asked Zuki.

'Old, old stories say was different, long time back. All one people. Big travel. Not now.'

The translation machine was having trouble finding the right words, making odd sounds as it searched for the correct translation.

'Ship carrier men – simple?' asked Zuki.

'Yes, simple people, many, many simple people, not clever.'

'Simple people happy?' asked Zuki.

The machine went 'beep'. The last word wasn't in the code list.

This was the first time Zuki had managed to extract so much information freely about the aliens, their captive always evading the questions by not understanding them.

And then Zuki produced the book, pushing it across the table to the alien.

It looked down at the book, hesitated a moment, and the opened the cover to expose the picture of the man holding the shining stone. Zuki looked closely at its face to see if there was any sign of recognition, but there were none.

The alien then turned the next page over, and this time there was a reaction – it moved its head back slightly, and the eyes narrowed.

'Where you get this?' came over the translator. Zuki told it.

'This like our language, many words the same, not all.'

Several more pages were turned over, the alien slowly shaking its head from side to side.

'Can you translate it for us?' asked Zuki.'

'Some words, not all – I not know them.' came the reply.

'We have copy of this book, you want to read it?' asked Zuki.

'Yes, I read.' The alien replied through the translator, and it looked up with nearest thing to eagerness Zuki had ever seen on its face.

'I leave you copy, you read. You tell us what you find?' asked Zuki.

'Yes.' it replied, nodding its head.

'Thank you,' said Zuki, 'we had good talk.' The alien nodded its head.

Brond was informed of the latest developments with regards to the alien and said, 'Well, that explains a few things. What do you make of the book having some of the same words the alien uses? I don't like the sound of that, or what it infers.'

'Could it possibly be that the race of people in the mountain are one and the same as the aliens?' asked Zuki, 'I know a lot of time has gone by, but the aliens seem different somehow, maybe it's the genetic modifications they have been doing.'

'Let's see what it makes of the book,' said Brond, 'that's if it will, and can translate it. Depends what it finds I suppose, as to whether it tells us anything we don't know.'

Next day, Brond and Zuki were just leaving one of the laboratories when a messenger came up to them,

'A man calling himself Rolic Pensling wishes to see you. He said it is very important, sir.'

'Right, send him to my office,' said Brond, 'and I'll meet him there.'

They got to the office just before their visitor, who swept into the room as if he knew where it was, and who would be in it.

The figure removed dark glasses, and then a wig of light brown hair, and smiled at them.

'The fewer people who know about this, the better.' said the Chief Councillor, 'I have decided to accept your offer of the crystal. The way things are moving at the moment, I need a little enhancing.'

Kono was called for.

'You and Zuki retrieve one of the boxes, please,' Brond said, passing something to Zuki.

They quickly returned with the crystal box and passed it to Brond.

'No, you administer the crystal, Zuki.' he said, 'If you would sit here sir, Kono will stand near you with his back to us, to catch you if you pass out. Are you sure you want to do this, sir?'

'Yes, I think it would be for the good of all.'

'Zuki will open the box and tilt it towards you,' said Brond, 'you must look directly at the crystal. When the light gets brighter, you will feel the urge to touch it, you must then do so. You will feel something like an electric shock, and you may well pass out. Kono will catch you and lay you on the floor until you come round, OK?'

'Yes.'

'Open the lid, Zuki.' Brond said firmly.

As the lid was opened, light shone out, lighting up the office and then it began to pulse slightly. Zuki was being reminded of his experience as a boy.

The intensity grew, the Chief Councillor leaned forward and touched the crystal and the blazing flash of light blinded them all. When their eyesight returned to near normal, Zuki looked in the box, exclaiming that the crystal had disappeared.

The Chief Councillor lay prone, hardly breathing for some twenty minutes, and Brond was beginning to get worried.

At last he stirred, and propped himself up on one elbow.

'I wouldn't like to do that every day,' he said, and then got shakily to his feet, helped by Kono.

'How do you feel, sir?' asked Brond.

'It might sound strange, but I feel more alive.' the Chief Councillor replied, 'My vision is better, well, sharper. Some of the things I was worried about seem to have disappeared – they are just a list of things that must be done. Thank you all.'

'I think that deserves a little celebration,' said Brond, reaching for a bottle and filling four glasses, 'here's to a new future for us all.'

That night the four of them 'hit the town,' the Chief Councillor in his dark glasses and wig.

Zuki received a call from the alien's compound.

'The men at the compound say the alien is asking for you.'

Zuki left a message for Brond because he couldn't find him and hastened over to see if his wildest dreams had come true. The usual greeting formalities over, Zuki asked:

'Did you read the book?'

'Yes,' came back, 'it difficult, some words not know.'

Over the next two hours, the basics of the story unfolded: -

Once there had been one race of people living in the temperate belt around the equator, but then a group who were keen to advance their knowledge scientifically broke away from the main more pastoral people, and tensions grew between them.

The scientists sought somewhere else to live, and an expedition crossed the desert and found the mountainous area, with a narrow belt of vegetation growing around its foot, and moved there.

A 'light stone' was found by one of them, and he became the new leader, and began the search for more 'light stones'. They found some, and they quickly advanced in their science.

Several years of huge dust storms drove them to seek shelter inside the mountain, and it was decided to find somewhere else to live – their only option was another world.

Two spaceships were developed, and most of them left, but a few felt it was too risky and stayed behind to eke out an existence outside the mountain after the storms abated.

'I think, you - me once one people, long, long time ago,' the translator said, 'another world not make same language as book – not happen.'

Zuki thanked the alien for its hard work, and reported back to Brond, who was not as astonished as Zuki thought he should be.

'I somehow sensed something like this,' Brond said, 'but not quite as it has unfolded. I wonder if we could risk a visit to the alien's planet. We have the ability now, and I know you are keen to return the alien to its people. I'll have a word with the Chief Councillor.'

It was later agreed that they could all go, including Kono, and Zuki rushed off to tell the alien. The only hint of surprise that Zuki could pick up was the alien sat bolt upright when he made the announcement, and then reached forward and placed its hand on Zuki's for a moment.

Two days later they set off for the space station, and then transferred to the main ship. She gently moved away from the station, set the co-ordinates, and then engaged the 'Star Drive' as they now called it. The stars blinked out of existence, and they were on their way.

As they approached the outer limits of the alien's star system they transmitted a message from the alien to its home world. It explained briefly what they had discovered about their distant cousins and Earth's hope for peace and co-operation. The alien pilot relayed information that could only be known by a native of the planet to aid the verification of their message. Finally, as a gift from Earth, five crystals were offered as a token of goodwill.

The wait for the round-trip of their radio message to and from the home world was almost unbearable. Added to that, the time it took for high level deliberations to either welcome them or vaporise them.

Eventually, the radio crackled and the reply filled the cramped cockpit. Zuki had heard enough of the Alien language to begin to understand a few words, but one word amongst the garble rang out clear... "FAMILY".

THE END

If you have enjoyed this book, please consider leaving a review on Amazon. It would mean a lot to us.

About the Author

"Back in 1998 I was commenting to a friend that I didn't go much on so called modern Science Fiction. It didn't seem as good or as interesting as the adventures stories written by the old masters of sci-fi – Clarke, Russell, Pohl, Asimov, Heinlein etc. His reaction was 'well, write your own then' – As I already had an idea at the back of my mind, I did. After printing up ten copies and binding them (hardback) they were passed around among like minded friends – and then came the request for more of the same! Again and again. Only one problem – I was spending too much time printing and binding and not writing, which I enjoy. Getting into 'print' is difficult – if not impossible – so I chose the 'eBook' route. I would recommend it to anyone who likes writing, and has a story to tell."

David (aka D.B) Reynolds-Moreton is a retired research and development engineer who lives in Devon, England with his wife. You can read a short biography of his life and adventures in science at :

www.sci-fi-cafe.com/david-reynolds-moreton